Heartless

A Star Is Dead

Jean Marie Stanberry

Published by Kingsmuir Press

Boston, Dundee, Auckland

http://www.jeanstanberry.com

Laying Low In Hollywood

One World United

The Illusion Of Order

Blood, Sweat and Fears

DEDICATION

Life is good. Who would have thought, many years ago, that I would be sitting here typing the dedication for my fifth book?

A dream that was realized not only through my own perseverance and dedication, but through the ceaseless support of so many people who have been in and out of my life.

Family, friends, co workers, teachers and clergy. My life has been shaped by so many people, in so many ways. I truly feel blessed by everyone who has touched my life in one way or another. Every one of you have taught me a lesson, good or bad, each lesson has caused me to grow in one way or another.

KINGSMUIR PRESS

This book is a work of fiction. Names, characters, businesses, places, events and incidents are either a figment of the author's imagination or used in a fictitious manner. Any resemblence to actual persons, living or dead or actual events is purely coincidental

The cover art is a composite of images by Toa55 and Aleksa D at FreeDigitalPhotos.net and they may not be reproduced in any manner without permission.

CHAPTER 1

It was going to be a hot one. It was barely eleven, yet it was already ninety-two degrees. All three major network meteorologists, with their virtual reality doppler weather maps touted the news that today would be the hottest day of the summer. Temperatures were slated to climb to just over one hundred degrees. Add to that the record high humidity and it was not much of a stretch of the imagination, to realize that the residents of the city of Chicago were going to be baking in their own huge, concrete and asphalt oven.

Unfortunately, it was going to be one of those days. It would be much too hot to play tennis. Hell, it was going to be so hot, it might even be too hot to lounge by the pool.

Sabine felt a cold chill run down the length of her spine. Her racing mind was trying to focus but the only thought she could focus on, was a saying that her own father had told her many years ago.

The sun, it seems so welcoming, beaming down on you from it's place in the sky, but sometimes the intense heat can change people, it can make them crazy, especially when extreme discomfort leads to desperation...

Sabine drew in a deep, shaky, breath and took a tiny, almost imperceptible step backwards. She was shaking her head slowly, her face was a mask of uncertainty. She had never been a religious person, but in the back of her mind she was vaguely realizing that she was silently repeating a prayer inside her head. "Please Lord, tell me that this is all just a bad dream."

Her heart was thudding loudly in her ears, like a deep base in rock concert that was way too loud. She was trying to stay calm but in moments she is fighting hysteria, it seems a struggle to merely breathe. Sabine realizes as she stands there, in moment of embarrassment, that she is still primly holding her teacup and saucer. This recent realization has caused her hands to begin to shaking uncontrollably.

She had already been rattled enough, the clattering of the teacup on it's little saucer was intensely annoying and suddenly she couldn't stand the sound another second. She nervously tried to set the teacup and it's saucer on the little table next to her, but being distracted like she was, she had misjudged the distance. The fine bone china teacup, with it's delicate pattern of violets, crashed to the floor.

Sabine looked down disjointedly at the teacup and her spilled tea. It seemed eerily irrational, but she couldn't help but smile to herself. She was actually relieved to see that the teacup was unharmed. It had landed on the thick wool oriental rug, though her mired brain reprimanded her briefly. At this point, why did she even care?

Perhaps it was because her beloved tea set had once belonged to her mother. Her mother had brought it from Europe herself in the early 1920's. She had packed it

2

carefully in the steamer trunk that crossed the Atlantic by ship. She had cherished the set all those years without so much as a chip in any of the pieces.

Sabine jumped a little bit as she was snapped abruptly back to reality by the angry voice of Karma. Apparently, a day of reckoning had arrived. Her dear departed mother had been a beautiful person, both inside and out. She had raised Sabine to be a kind and gentle person and she had been, for a while. Sabine couldn't help but wonder when she had changed. When had she become this horrible person?

Sabine sighed with regret. It was true, she had not conducted herself as elegantly as she had led on to everyone all these years. In her young adult years, she had been completely out of control. None of that had been elegant at all. The drinking, the sex, the drugs. Her mother wouldn't have allowed any of it. No way, her mother was as classy as they came, she wouldn't have liked young Sabine one bit.

Now it seems that Karma had finally come to settle the score and Sabine would pay for all the pain that she had inflicted on others over the years, or so that is what Karma had told her was going to happen.

Sabine tried to swallow, but her throat was dry, like sandpaper. She was fighting panic, this could not possibly be happening, she thought to herself. Her mind was racing in a hundred different directions. Was this what people meant, when they felt as if their life had flashed before their eyes? It seemed as if every joyous, and every dark, forgotten memory had somehow fought it's way to the forefront of her brain. This was utter madness!

She giggled a nervous giggle, the kind of laugh that comes out when you sincerely hope someone is joking with you, but deep down in the pit of your stomach, you know that they're not. Sabine was realizing as the seconds ticked by, that this was not a joke, and it was not a nightmare she could simply wake up from. This was real, this was the end.

Sabine struggled to compose herself as she took another uncertain step backwards. Her body was slowly succumbing to the panic and she was feeling strangely lightheaded. Her heart rate had suddenly doubled in the last thirty seconds and she could feel beads of sweat coursing their way slowly down her back.

The adrenaline surging through her body was commanding her to run away, but there was nowhere to go, she was trapped. It was just like her life and the culmination of her lies, there was no way out.

Sabine felt remarkably naive, she had deliberately placed her chair there in the corner of the room because this was her domain, she had felt comfortable, not threatened. She hadn't planned to entertain Karma long, a cup of tea, a lame apology and she would thrust this inconvenient guest out.

Unfortunately, this encounter hadn't gone as she had planned. She had felt safe here, this was her own home.

She had never sensed the danger, she had trusted Karma, but that had been foolish and proud. Now there was no escape.

Sabine struggled to draw in a breath, she could feel her body succumbing to the apprehensive shaking. Her legs were getting weaker by the second and they threatened to buckle and give out underneath her. Her overloaded mind was racing back through the years of her life, she was painfully aware, this was the end...

She cleared her throat to speak, but there was nothing she could say that would undo the past. Sabine had lived her life exactly as she had pleased, never caring who she had hurt as she pushed her way up the ladder to stardom. Now it was too late, feelings had been hurt, lives had been irreparably damaged, her ruthlessness had taken it's toll, now Karma seemed to be laughing in her face, taunting her.

She couldn't deny it, she had been selfish, she had left a trail of carnage in her wake, but surely...surely it wasn't so bad that she deserved to die. She was a star for Pete's sake, she had thousands of fans. Did it really have to end this way?

Of course, Sabine was in denial. She had always believed she was immune to the horrors of the outside world. She was a goddess, people worshipped her. She was the great Sabine Rousseau, people stood in line for hours just to get her autograph. Why would one person believe that they had the power to end it all?

"Wait!" cried Sabine, her voice shaking in fear. "My checkbook is in the bureau drawer, I can write you a check, just tell me how much you want. I can help you...please, just tell me what you want."

Karma just shook it's head slowly. Karma had no need for money. Of course, money cannot buy back a lifetime of selfish and foolish deeds. Karma was now done talking, Karma was approaching her now.

Sabine was consumed with panic, tears were coursing down her cheeks and she was struggling to breathe as her blind, angry, justice approached her swiftly. She felt the rapid blow of the knife, but there was no pain as Karma plunged it deeply into her chest. This must be a dream, a nightmare really, because it couldn't possibly be real...there was no pain...

The knife plunged into her chest infused with a mixture of passion and hatred. It seemed surreal, the knife plunged into her chest again and again, Sabine didn't even try to count the blows or attempt to absorb the pain and hatred in the eyes of her attacker.

Sabine searched for an emotion, but felt none. As the moments ticked by, she began to feel the pain that she had so carelessly inflicted on others for so many years.

The room seemed to tilt and bend crazily. The moments seemed to be passing in slow motion, it was as if she had been drugged. Sabine was suddenly angry as she watched the spray of blood arcing across the wall of her study. She wanted to shout and curse at her assailant, but nothing would come out of her mouth. Her words were consumed by the sucking chest wounds, her assailant had already inflicted on her.

She wanted to shout at Karma what a mess it had made. It was horrible, the wall of the study, the expensive oriental rug, her designer silk blouse. Who would pay for all this? Sabine let her body slide slowly down the wall, her legs could not hold her body weight any longer. Her eyes were narrowed in anger. Karma had made a terrible mess!

Sabine could feel her head swimming, her vision was getting blurrier, she realized that for some reason, she was now sitting on the floor with her back against the wall. The walls were curving inward and the room seemed to be enveloped in a thick fog. Sabine squeezed her eyes closed in an attempt to shake off her stupor. She looked up in awe, at her assailant's face, which was now smiling. Inexplicably, the room seemed to be growing dimmer with each passing moment.

Suddenly, Harvey is standing there in front of her, holding his hand out to her. Sabine manages to give him a surprised smile. Harvey was the one person who had truly adored her.

Sabine struggles to reach out and take Harvey's hand. She stretches, but she cannot quite reach his hand. The room seems to be rolling and tilting and she suddenly has the overwhelming urge to lay down.

Why do I feel so weak? She asks herself. Harvey is right there. In moments, her mind clears and she realizes with complete clarity what has happened. She has been stabbed. Her wounds are fatal, blood is pumping relentlessly out of her chest.

Sabine decides this must be a dream...why else would Harvey be there, offering his hand to her? That's it, this is nothing but a terrible nightmare, a surreal dream that Karma has come to her and exacted it's revenge. It cannot possibly be true that her life is draining slowly from her body.

Harvey is frowning, he shakes his head slowly. Sabine inches her elegantly manicured hand up her body to clutch her chest wound. With each beat of her heart, she can feel the warm stickiness of her own blood, surging out of her chest and ruining her six hundred dollar, designer silk blouse.

She shakes her head weakly in disgust, a six hundred dollar blouse! Her mind is growing foggy, but still she clings to her theory that this most certainly is a nightmare, this could not possibly be happening to her.

Sabine's entire body is shaking uselessly, she is struggling in vain to keep her head, which seems to be getting heavier by the moment, off the floor. She was a star, it wouldn't be respectable to be found laying on the floor. Karma is standing over her, smiling. Sabine struggles to say something, anything, to make this madness stop, but her chest wounds will not allow her to draw in enough breath to say anything at all.

She is suddenly aware that Harvey has arrived to bring her home with him. She is not afraid any more, she is going to join him, they will be together again. Sabine reaches out to take Harvey's hand as she sputters out her last breath. She finally rests her head on the soft wool of the antique oriental rug. Her consciousness fades away slowly, she feels herself drifting into a cool mist, sounds around her fading, the light is fading. All is now peaceful and quiet...

Chapter 2

Detective Doug Bellamy glances around in awe as he pulls his navy blue, unmarked police car through the heavy, wrought iron gates of the imposing, stone mansion. The fading afternoon sun is filtering down through the dark green canopy of towering oaks and maples, their regal branches swaying in the slight breeze creating a kaleidoscope of light that seems to dance across the long, curving, brick driveway. The scene might have seemed majestic to him, had he not already known of the horrors that lay within the elegant home.

The call had come out to him less than ten minutes ago and the heart wrenching shock and dismay he had felt when he received the call still overwhelmed his body and mind. It all seemed so senseless. At this point, he knew what had happened, though the reality of her death wouldn't sink in until he actually saw her body.

He cruises slowly down the sweeping brick driveway, his eyes taking in every tiny detail. He was subconsciously making mental notes to himself as he approached the stately manor. There were already three other police vehicles parked in the drive and the coroner's van was backed conspicuously up to the front door, it's doors flung wide open to receive yet another victim. His heart is heavy with regret, there is no mistaking that something horrible has happened here, even though the gravity of it all has not yet consumed him.

Bellamy pulls his car up behind the other three police cruisers and parks it there in the sun dappled shade. He jogs quickly up the curved stone stairs of the mansion. He is so focused on the task that lies ahead of him, he is barely aware that his partner, Chris Salazar is trotting up the stairs right behind him.

The heavy, mahogany front door with it's ornate panel of leaded glass, is standing wide open. Bellamy glances it over quickly as he walks through, assessing it for any damage. The door and it's frame appear to be completely undamaged. He makes a mental note, there seems to be no evidence that it has been forced open.

Bellamy's trained eyes glance around the elegant, gleaming foyer. This wasn't, what he would call, a routine crime scene. He was used to the seedier side of town with the drive by shootings, back alley murders and domestic quarrels gone wrong in low income housing.

This was different, the rich tended to end their arguments with lawsuits, not weapons. This was most likely a crime of passion, not desperation.

The foyer is expansive and echoing, a full two stories tall. Light from the windows on the second floor filtered down in long shafts to the foyer's shining marble floor. Bellamy watches numbly as dust particles drift slowly down through the bright column of light. The gleaming marble floor is spotless, the heavy antique furnishings and the carefully placed accessories seem to be untouched, not hinting at all to the atrocities that lay just beyond this tidy foyer.

Bellamy stood there for a few moments gazing around and listening, he is pretending that he is getting a feel for the place and collecting his thoughts, but he is really preparing himself for the sight of the body. It was something he can never quite get used to.

When the dispatcher read off the address to him, he had thought there must be some mistake. He was still slightly in shock, even as he had pulled into the driveway. It was all he could do but hope that it wasn't her.

Salazar had already grown bored and pushed ahead, he was already migrating towards the sounds of their crime scene. Bellamy could hear the buzz of voices coming from the study, which sat just to the right of the foyer. He reluctantly ambled that direction, apprehensive of what he would see when he entered the room. Of course, nobody loved a murder scene, but when it involved someone you felt a connection with, it made it that much worse.

Bellamy had nearly twenty years of experience with the Chicago Police force and he had more than ten years in the homicide division. He had worked plenty of murder cases in his day but he never got used to the initial shock he felt when he first walked in the room or arrived on the scene of a murder.

The thing he could never seem to get over, is how cruel the world seemed to be turning as the years passed by. He could understand the passion involved in the actual murder, but when people tortured and maimed and then murdered their victims, it seemed as if the world was loosing it's respect for life itself.

Bellamy ambled slowly into the study, his eyes searching for anything out of the ordinary, his partner Chris Salazar was already there, silently snapping photos.

The two detectives were a well matched team, despite the fact that there was nearly twenty years difference in their ages. Bellamy and Salazar had been partners for more than five years, they complimented each other perfectly, what small detail one missed, the other picked up. Their styles were perfectly suited and they made an ideal team. Bellamy was older and more experienced, while Chris Salazar was younger and more enthusiastic.

Bellamy was tall and lean with thick brown hair that had recently become peppered with silver. His kind eyes and angular face made him quite handsome for his age.

He always smiled when he thought about it. At some point in the past ten years, he had gone from being the department heartthrob to a distinguished, older gentleman. Bellamy wasn't sure when this transformation had taken place, but it seemed to him as if it had happened overnight.

When he had started in homicide he had spent the better part of his career fending off the various women who hit on him. It seems there were quite a few woman who were attracted to a man in a position of authority, even though he had told them all he was happily married. Back then he'd been the youngster in homicide, at least till his partner Van Roode retired five years ago and he was paired with the new department heartthrob, Chris Salazar.

His partner Salazar was young, in his mid twenties. He owed his own rugged good looks to his hispanic father, who he had never even met. His mother had met Salazar's father while they were both working on a cruise ship, he was a mechanic, she was a nurse. The two began a whirlwind romance, then she found out she was pregnant. She told her lover, thinking he would be happy, but he got off the ship and she never saw him again. She was forced to raise Chris as a single mother. She returned to her hometown of Chicago, took a job in a hospital and eventually married, giving Chris two younger siblings.

The women of Chicago seemed to find Salazar completely irresistible. He was olive skinned, with a mass of rippling muscles which he liked to show off with tight t-shirts when he was off duty. He considered himself to be quite the ladies man and of course, he truly was. He never seemed to be without a new, gorgeous woman on his arm.

The partners were both walking carefully around the study, which was a flurry of activity. The coroner and the crime scene investigators were already hard at work. The entire house was considered the crime scene, but this particular room, being the scene of the murder, was being dissected for the most minute pieces of evidence.

It was a lot of work, but when a murder finally went to trial the jury had to be convinced beyond a reasonable doubt. Most recently, proving a case relied heavily on science, and for good reason...science doesn't lie. It is consistent, reliable, unemotional.

Relying on humans, who are full of faults, is risky. Over time, witnesses become more and more unsure of what they have seen, suspects may be expert liars and able to sway a jury, even choice of lawyer can affect a case. That is what makes a thorough crime scene investigation so important. Following hard evidence leads to a fool proof conviction.

Suspects can leave their mark behind in many ways and it is up to the CSI's to find any bit of evidence the killer left behind at the scene or on their victim.

Murder weapons, fingerprints and DNA. These are things that are all important to the prosecution. It was Bellamy's job to recreate the crime scene for the jury, sometimes years later, when everyone's memory of the day had faded. Things that seemed to leave an indelible impression today, never seem as clear and convincing years later, when they were revisited.

Bellamy surveys the room carefully, it looks like an intricate road map, even the tiniest bits of potential evidence have all been flagged with yellow marking devices, and the CSI's are busily taking photos of every possible view of the crime scene.

The medical examiner, Brad Denning, is kneeling over the body, he has a magnifying glass and is inspecting a mark on the victim's face. When he sees the detectives coming into the room, he gives them both a wry smile. The three of them are friends, so he is happy to see them, though they prefer to play a round of golf or meet for drinks over chewing the fat at the scene of a horrific murder.

"Hey, Doug, Chris," he says, standing up, stretching his legs and acknowledging the two men.

"Hey Brad," said Doug Bellamy, his voice is coarse with emotion, as he finally gets his first glance of the victim's body. As he'd predicted, it is just as horrendous as he had imagined it would be. Unfortunately, the shock of seeing a dead body is something you never really got used to, even after years in homicide. It was especially unsettling, when it was someone you recognized.

Bellamy's trained eyes flicker across the room taking in the entire scene, he is frowning in bewilderment, something is not right. The victim is bathed in blood, literally from the chest down, and she is sprawled unnaturally on the expensive oriental rug. He takes a few careful steps, a bit closer to the body, his eyes assessing the entire scene carefully.

His eyes wander to a pattern of arterial blood spray, arcing across the back corner of the wall, indicating that the woman had been standing and pretty much trapped in the corner when she had been attacked. Remarkably, the rest of the room seemed pretty much untouched. It was particularly noteworthy that there were no obvious signs of a struggle. The victim must have been drugged or completely subdued, Bellamy thought to himself.

"It's a damn shame guys. She was such a beautiful, talented woman, yet whoever did this, was completely consumed with anger," said Brad, his face was grim.

"Any theories about what may have happened?" asked Chris, kneeling down to take a closer look at the body. The woman was older, but still quite beautiful. Her hair was elegantly coiffed and her makeup was meticulously applied. It was obvious she had money, she was dressed elegantly, and except for what appeared to be a small bruised area on her left cheek, the room gave no indication that there had even been a struggle, a sure sign in his mind, that she had been familiar with her attacker.

Bellamy is standing there with his arms folded over his chest as he looks the victim over carefully. The arterial spray on the back wall of the room and the pattern of blood trailing down the wall indicates that the woman had been standing near the wall when she was stabbed, she obviously fell back against the wall, eventually sliding down the wall, to the floor. The position of the body now didn't support that. She had been moved, either by her assailant or the crime scene team.

The woman's ivory, silk blouse, was stained a dark red with her blood and Bellamy didn't need the medical examiner to tell him that she had been stabbed multiple times. He noticed that her blouse had been completely unbuttoned, but it had been pulled back across her chest. Bellamy was making a mental note to self that most likely someone had redressed the body after she was dead. He was assuming that there had been a sexual assault.

The blood surrounding the body had already soaked into the rug, creating a dark red aura around the body that seemed to barely obscure the bold pattern in the thick, wool rug.

"Well, my guess is that someone came for a civilized cup of tea and left far less civilized," said Brad, raising his eyebrows at the two men.

"How long has she been dead?" asked Chris Salazar.

"My best guess, factoring in the room temp and everything else, is that she died sometime late this morning," said Denning.

"She was stabbed then?" asked Bellamy.

"Yes, it appears she was stabbed multiple times, so I want to say that her cause of death is exsanguination from multiple stab wounds, but of course, I want to wait for the tox screens and blood work before I commit to anything.

I am assuming she knew her assailant since there was seemingly, no signs of a struggle. But of course, it's also possible she might have been drugged or even possibly suffering from some sort of a medical condition, like a heart attack. I mean, who just stands there and lets someone stab them to death? I'm guessing that her guest this morning was someone she trusted, or at least had no fear of. I'm assuming she was completely taken by surprise when the weapon came out," said Denning.

"Have we found the murder weapon?" asked Salazar, his eyes still roaming the room, checking every small detail.

"No, we haven't found the murder weapon, but we've only just begun. I mean look at this place, the house is huge, and it sits on just over three acres so the murder weapon could be anywhere on the grounds. I'm guessing, whomever did this took the murder weapon with them. All these freakin crime shows are killing us. They're giving the bad guys all kinds of helpful tips. I mean they pretty much spell it out to these losers what they can do to make it more difficult for us. Get rid of the weapon, wear gloves so you won't leave fingerprints, I mean shit, give me a break!" complained Denning.

"Yeah, I know," rued Bellamy.

"So far the CSI's haven't found anything on the premises, but like I said, it's a massive search area, and so far they've really only had the chance to go over this room," said Denning, shrugging.

"I'll have them check trash cans and dumpsters in a one mile radius, just in case our perp ditched the weapon somewhere," said Bellamy.

Bellamy grabs a pair of latex gloves from Denning's case and pulls them on. He carefully picks up one of the woman's meticulously manicured hands and turns it over in his own. It looks perfect, there are no defensive wounds on her hands, no broken nails, not a speck of dirt. No sign whatsoever, of a struggle.

"I want her hands bagged, and I want her checked for trace, in case there was a struggle. Maybe she was tazed, or drugged. Our perp had to leave something behind," said Bellamy, tilting his head to the side thoughtfully, as he assessed the victim.

"Of course Doug, like always," said the medical examiner, nodding to him.

"All right, I want to have a look around," said Bellamy, peeling off the gloves and standing up.

"Hold on there a second, I do have something interesting to point out that I believe you will find quite fascinating," said Denning, flashing him a sly smile.

"What's that?" asked Bellamy, stopping and staring at the medical examiner intently.

"There is one thing that makes this murder unique and a bit scary, if I do say so. It is something I haven't seen personally in my career, but I have heard of it. It brings a whole new dimension in regards to the amount of passion exhibited by our assailant," said Denning.

"What's that?" asked Bellamy, the medical examiner suddenly had his undivided attention.

"In addition to her multiple stab wounds, whoever did this, opened her chest cavity, removed her heart and apparently took it with them," said Denning, raising his eyebrows at them.

"You're kidding me...right?" cried Salazar, unable to believe it was true. It was shocking, it almost seemed like something you would see in some crazy slasher movie, not something you would witness in a high class neighborhood like this.

Bellamy was stunned, he just stood there gaping at the medical examiner in shock. He had been doing homicide for more than ten years, he had seen enough murders in his lifetime to understand the passion involved in the actual murder.

Human beings were complex animals, passion expressed in love, lust, anger and hatred were all closely related. Relationships had their ups and downs and sometimes misunderstandings, betrayals, or even a lifetime of pain, cumulated in an unfortunate murder.

He almost shivered when he thought about someone cutting another person's heart out. What kind of person could actually do that? Take out a knife and actually cut out someone's heart? It would be time consuming and someone would have to be so emotionally removed...so heartless themselves. Or maybe the killer was sending them a message. Maybe whomever did this was sending the message that they believed that the victim had no heart.

"I can only wish that I was joking, but it is true. Whoever murdered Ms. Rousseau, seems to have had a deeply rooted hatred for her. So deeply rooted, they actually stole her heart."

Bellamy walked back over and knelt near the woman's head and looked the body over carefully. Her aged face was carefully made up, her mascara wasn't running all over her face as if she'd been in an emotional argument. Had she shown any sort of emotion towards her attacker? Her ice blue eyes were staring and vacant, Bellamy stares into them numbly, as if they are beaconing to him. The medical examiner leans over and carefully presses her eyelids closed, then he gently places her arms at her sides. Finally, the woman looks at peace.

"The photos are all done, the scene is all yours," says Denning, standing up and closing the latches on his case.

"Hmmmm," grunted Bellamy, seemingly incapable of speech.

"Hey, you OK Bellamy?" asks Denning. Bellamy seems lost, deep in thought.

"Yeah, I'm fine. I guess I'm still in shock, it just seems surreal. Sabine Rousseau, I can't believe it's really her," he said, sighing, as he drags his eyes away from her.

"I know, I was heartbroken when I got the call. I was a huge fan, I think I saw every one of her movies when I was a kid. In fact, when I was sixteen I secretly had a crush on her daughter. What was her name? You know, the pretty one.

She was in a couple of movies and she was going to marry Gerard Renoir," said Brad.

"Hmmm, I don't remember the daughter too much from the movies, I don't think any of her movies did that well. I just remember all the hoopla when she was engaged to the British Earl, or whatever the hell he was. You remember that silly scandal, don't you? She ran away with some other guy and broke off the engagement. My mother was so upset about it, you'd think it was her own daughter who had completely lost her mind," said Bellamy, laughing at the memory.

"Yeah, I remember. Actually, I wouldn't be surprised if Rousseau had planned that little fiasco herself. You know, at the time she was getting older and she hadn't had a movie role in eons. She was no longer in the spotlight. What better way to end up back in the spotlight, than to have a huge family drama?" said Brad Denning, raising his eyebrows playfully.

"Well she's back in the spotlight again, though this time she can't enjoy it. It's just a shame, she was such a talented woman. My mother completely worshipped her, I can't tell you how many times she dragged my father and I to the ballet, just to see her. She was beautiful," said Bellamy, shaking his head miserably.

"She's still beautiful, her driver's license states she's sixty six years old, but I don't think she looks a day over fifty," said Denning.

Salazar was still walking slowly around the room, taking notes, making a mental image of everything he saw there, what seemed right with the room, what seemed out of place.

Unfortunately, there wasn't much to note, the room was clean and everything seemed to be in it's place. Two leather, wing back chairs had been pulled up to a table by the bay window and there was a tray carefully arranged with a teapot made of exquisite bone china. There was also a tiny bowl with lemon slices, which were now starting to shrivel and dry out. Also on the tray was a tiny china pitcher with now curdled cream, and a sugar bowl. There were two silver spoons with elegantly folded linen napkins, virtually untouched on the tray. One teacup sat on the table, filled with tea, literally untouched. The other teacup had fallen to the floor and spilled near Sabine's body.

"So this lady was like a ballet dancer or something?" asked Salazar. Obviously, he was a bit intrigued, he had just caught the tail end of the conversation.

"She was one of the greatest ballet dancers ever! Her name is Sabine Rousseau, she was a great legend in her day," said Denning wistfully, he appeared to be deep in thought.

"Yeah, OK," said Salazar, with a bit of a shrug, he had never followed dancing of any sort and he didn't plan on following it now. The ballet did not interest him at all, he thought it was all kind of gay, everyone prancing around in leotards. Of course, a big, manly man like him would never be caught dead watching the ballet.

He ambled across the room to take a look at an assortment of gilded framed photos that had been meticulously arranged on a walnut console in the corner of the room There were photos of Sabine with her kids at the beach, a photo taken in Paris near the Eiffel tower, a few photos obviously taken on a sailboat, and an old black and white photo of Sabine in her younger years, pirouetting for the camera. Salazar leaned over to get a closer look at it.

"Hmmm, not half bad," said Salazar, as he glanced at her picture. "I can see she was a hot little number back in her day."

"Back in her day Sabine Rousseau was elegant and refined. She wasn't a bimbo, like all the Hollywood sluts everyone seems to worship these days," said Bellamy, rolling his eyes.

"Hey, I just said she was hot, you know, nice body and all," said Salazar, frowning and shaking his head miserably. He hoped that Bellamy's nostalgic affection for their victim wouldn't cloud his judgement in their investigation of her murder.

Salazar was worried, Bellamy never showed any emotion. Besides, it was a policy. When people had a personal relationship with the victim, they weren't allowed to work the case. Salazar was well aware that Bellamy had no relationship with Sabine Rousseau, in fact, he was almost certain he had never even met the woman. Yet he had just defended her honor, when he truly had no reason to defend her.

Sabine Rousseau had been a public figure and Salazar knew that many public figures were not what they appeared to be to their adoring fans. Many lived more than one life, one that was respectable, the perfect face they showed to the world. The other was darker, not always pretty, it was a life that most people never knew exsisted.

"What else can you tell me Brad? Did you find any evidence of a sexual assault?" asked Bellamy.

"Well, I'll know more when I get her back to the morgue and do my full examination. I can tell you that the body had been moved. It was pulled away from the wall to where it is now and there was evidence of a redress.

Her blouse had been opened and her bra had been sliced through, but I'm guessing that was for the sole purpose of cutting her heart out. Then whoever did it, pulled her blouse back over her breasts, more to conceal the shock of her gaping chest wound, than to protect the victim's modesty, I'm guessing. Also, her panties were pulled up haphazardly, in a way that seemed unnatural, so of course, I will do a full sexual assault kit and swab for semen," said Denning.

"We'll be waiting to hear from you," said Bellamy, already looking around, trying to decide where he would head off to next.

"OK guys, I'm out of here," said Denning, pulling his latex gloves off and wading them up.

"Okay Brad, thanks. Hey, do you happen to know who found her?" asked Bellamy.

"Yeah, it was her youngest daughter Patrice. She lives here at the mansion with her. The uniforms took her out to the patio. She got all high and mighty with them and was refusing to leave the house. She's a bit odd. I hope you have better luck with her, than the first guys on the scene did, she wasn't making a whole lot of sense earlier. Though I'm not sure it's even possible, I'm getting the feeling the daughter is a bit of a whack job," said Denning.

"What do you mean?" asked Bellamy.

"You'll figure it out when you talk to her. I mean the girl is like twenty four years old and she still lives here with Mommy. I guess Sabine has two other children but they are both quite a bit older, neither of them lives anywhere nearby and they are apparently estranged from the family.

There's no husband in the picture, you remember, the great Harvey Bernard passed away a couple of years ago. Ms. Rousseau has been widowed for just over two years," said Denning, with a little shrug.

"Thanks Brad, I think I'll go to go out to the patio and have a little talk with the daughter," said Bellamy, heading toward the back of the house.

Chapter 3

Bellamy was walking slowly down the long, sparkling hallway, his eyes darting back and forth, taking in every detail as he walked along. The mansion was large and elegantly furnished. Everything seemed to be perfect, nothing was out of place. That in itself, was completely creeping him out. To Bellamy, the mansion had no personality. It wasn't homey at all, it seemed cold and sterile. He couldn't imagine living in a house so large and impersonal. It seemed like an awful lot of house for a reclusive older woman and her only remaining daughter. There wasn't even any evidence that they had any pets.

Bellamy ambled slowly through the kitchen. It was expansive and open with large bowed windows that overlooked the massive yard and pool area. The kitchen was gleaming and spotless like the rest of the house, not so much as a dirty dish in the sink. The wide expanses of expensive Carrara marble countertops were wiped down and virtually empty of any clutter, there wasn't so much as a utility bill, to hint that people might actually inhabit this house. It was strangely lifeless, like a display home. Bellamy was silently wondering if Rousseau and her daughter were both a bit OCD or maybe they just ate out a lot. He walked over to the large, built-in refrigerator and stuck his head in.

He was amazed to see a wide assortment of fruits and vegetables in the drawers. The shelves were well stocked with organic milk and yogurt and there were neatly stacked plastic containers, all carefully labeled with contents and dates of purchase, containing fish and chicken. He almost chuckled to himself. Ms. Rousseau was definitely OCD. As a dancer, she was probably compulsively concerned about her weight. He wouldn't be surprised, if she'd never had a taste of junk food in her entire life.

"Can I help you?" asked a sultry female voice.

Detective Bellamy wheeled around quickly in surprise, he was staring at the woman who was standing there behind him, assessing him cooly.

"I'm Detective Bellamy, I was just having a look around. Who are you?" he snapped, almost shrinking away in embarrassment.

He was feeling very uncomfortable, this woman had abruptly placed her huge frame in his personal space and it was making him anxious. Bellamy had a comfort zone and this woman had set off his personal alarm. She was standing much too close, and he could feel his hand slowly inching toward his gun at his waist.

"I am Sabine's daughter, Patrice Bernard, I live here. Did you find what you were looking for in there?" she asked, raising her eyebrows at him.

"Actually, I was looking for you," said Bellamy, managing to take an uncomfortable step backward. Now his body was really more in the refrigerator, than out.

"I hate to tell you sir, but it has been quite a few years since I've been able to fit in there," she said, flashing him a sly grin.

Bellamy resisted the urge to roll his eyes, this woman didn't strike him as a typical, grieving daughter. Of course, he hadn't expected Patrice to be typical at all, in fact, he had already been forewarned.

He had anticipated that, like most people who found a family member's body, that Sabine's daughter would be an emotional train wreck. Instead, it almost seemed as if she was flirting with him. He looked her over carefully, he guessed that she worked full time, her clothing was professional and obviously expensive. She was wearing a pale yellow linen suit and white leather flats, her curly blond hair was swept back in a large clip with a few errant strands falling around her face. He watched as her eyes flickered over him dully, as she seemed to be sizing him up as well.

She wasn't really what he had expected, being Sabine Rousseau's daughter. Sabine was an average height, but Patrice was quite tall, he was guessing she was at least six feet tall, and he was sure she outweighed him by at least seventy pounds. He couldn't help but feel uncomfortable, the way she was standing much too close to him. She had folded her arms across her chest and was staring at him, her gaze was unwavering. Bellamy didn't like being backed into a corner, he closed the refrigerator door and took two uncomfortable steps to his left, merely for the sake of putting a bit of distance between him and Patrice.

He was still searching her face for any signs that she was grieving her mother's death. Her face was mostly expressionless, though her eyes were red and she looked as if she'd been crying.

Though this woman had Sabine's ice blue eyes and pale blonde hair, it seemed as if that was where the resemblance ended. Sabine was average in height, maybe five foot six and she was thin and very fit, even for a woman of sixty six. Her daughter though, was quite heavy, Bellamy guessed that she was probably at least, eighty to ninety pounds overweight.

"It is very nice to meet you Miss Bernard, is there somewhere we can talk?" he asked. "You do realize that you are not allowed to be in the house while the investigation is going on?"

"We can go back out to the terrace. I would much rather be out there anyway. I can't bear to hear the things they are saying about my mother," she said, nearly breaking down in tears again.

"Was someone being disrespectful?" asked Bellamy, almost horrified by the very thought. The entire staff was taught to respect the dead, he wanted to be informed if there was someone on the team who was behaving unprofessionally.

"No, they were all just doing their jobs, I just can't bare

the thought that she is gone, to hear them talk about the time of death, and things like that was really shaking me up," whimpered Patrice.

Bellamy followed her out to the terrace and pulled up one of the heavy wrought iron chairs next to her. The expansive stone terrace was mostly shaded by the thick canopy of trees and it overlooked a large grecian pool and the rest of the perfectly manicured gardens that surrounded the mansion.

"You have a very beautiful home Miss Bernard," said Bellamy, carefully trying to get her to start talking.

"Yes," she whispered, she was staring at him, her gaze was unwavering. It unnerved him a little bit. She was definitely not a typical grieving family member.

"This seems like a lot of house for you and your mother, I imagine it is very expensive to maintain. Did your mother ever consider downsizing?" asked Bellamy. He wasn't sure why he had asked that, he just wondered sometimes, if some people didn't have an unlimited amount of money. Sabine Rousseau had been a huge star in her time, but she hadn't been in a movie since the 1970's and he hadn't really heard much about her at all in at least twenty years.

"This was my grandfather's estate, my mother inherited it. Since my father died, she's been saying she wanted to sell the place, it truly is too big for just the two of us, but we have so many fond memories here, she couldn't bare to part with it. Besides, the money is not an issue, my father left us well provided for," sighed Patrice, her eyes were now far away, in thought.

"That's right, Harvey Bernard was your father," said Bellamy, surprised that he had nearly forgot that small detail.

"My father was one of the highest paid, leading male actors ever! Besides, he made plenty of shrewd investments, he wanted his family well provided for after he was gone, he didn't want my mother to have to leave the home that she loved," said Patrice.

"Tell me, when was the last time you saw your mother alive?" asked Bellamy.

"I have been busy, I hadn't seen her since yesterday morning, before I left for work," said Patrice.

"Do you know, did your mother have any plans for the day today? Was she planning on having any guests?" asked Bellamy, hoping that maybe Patrice knew who her mother had planned to spend her day with.

"I'm not really sure what she had planned, probably tennis," said Patrice, distractedly. She was inspecting her manicure distastefully.

"Where?"

"Here, the tennis court is down that path, behind the pool house," said Patrice, waving her hand haphazardly in the direction of the curving brick path. Bellamy gave her a blank stare. It was frustrating, he couldn't read her she seemed so unmoved, her voice was emotionless, unwavering. Not what he expected of someone who's mother had just been brutally murdered in her own home.

"Did she have friends that came by? Who would she have played tennis with if you were at work?" asked Bellamy, trying to pry any small detail out of this woman, who seemed to be a bit of a closed book at the moment.

"I don't play tennis, not that she didn't try to make an athlete out of me. She got me lessons, the whole nine yards. To put it mildly, I suck at tennis and she's always hated to play with me. It was never been much of a challenge for her. She really didn't have friends that came by at least, not anymore. The only person she ever played tennis with was her personal trainer, Steve," said Patrice, sighing in boredom.

"Excellent, how can I get in touch with Steve?" asked Bellamy, jotting a few notes on his notepad.

"I don't know," sighed Patrice, still assessing her nails wearily.

"Can you tell me, what is Steve's last name?" asked Bellamy, trying hard to conceal his impatience. He was starting to get a little miffed. Patrice's mother was dead and she was holding out on him, he could feel it.

"Detective, perhaps you don't realize this, but I have my own life. I am very busy. I cannot be expected to know every single detail of my mother's life. All I know is the man's name is Steve. I have a career, I'm not here during the day, I've only met the man once!" she cried, surprising him with her sudden burst of emotion.

Bellamy gave her a stunned look, her eyes were flashing with barely concealed anger and her face was suddenly flushed with emotion. For some reason, the very mention of her mother's personal trainer had angered her. Bellamy decided that he would look into the personal trainer later, it seemed this topic of conversation was a bit of a sore subject for Patrice. He took a deep breath and decided to take his questions in a different direction.

"I'm very sorry Ms. Bernard. Why don't you tell me a little bit about yourself? Where do you work?" asked Bellamy, still gazing around in awe at the spectacular gardens.

Patrice smiled at him, pleased that he seemed to be interested in her. "I'm a professor at the college, I teach world history. I specialize in Egyptian history. Do you like Egyptian history Detective Bellamy?" asked Patrice, flashing him a slightly seductive smile.

"I find all sorts of history fascinating, but we aren't talking about me, we are talking about you," said Bellamy, nervously trying to get her back on track.

"I would much rather talk about you detective. Are you married?" asked Patrice, her voice was dripping with honey.

"Ms. Bernard, do I need to remind you that this is a murder investigation? I need you to focus, please. What time did you get done at the college yesterday?" asked Bellamy.

"You can call me Patrice, and you never answered my question," she said, smiling at him coyly. Bellamy sighed in resignation and resisted the urge to roll his eyes. Patrice Bernard was completely inappropriate, he doubted she would be of any use to him at all in his investigation.

"Yes, I am married, now will you answer my question please!" he cried angrily, he could feel the perspiration on his brow, she was totally messing with him!

"My classes were done by three thirty, but I was in my office till nearly six, reading and grading research papers. So Detective, would you call yourself happily married?" crooned Patrice, giving him a sly smile and leaning back in her chair, stretching her back seductively.

"Did you come back here then?" asked Bellamy, ignoring her question about the status of his marriage. Her behavior was completely inappropriate, especially for someone who had just found their mother's murdered body.

"No, I went to class," said Patrice, licking her lips seductively, she was staring him down boldly. Bellamy looked away nervously. If she was trying to intimidate him, it was working and he wasn't sure why. This chick was something else.

"You didn't answer my question, so I'll assume the answer is not happy. You've been married quite awhile, I'd guess," crooned Patrice, flashing him a sly smile.

"Miss Bernard, my marriage is not on the table for discussion, are we clear? I am investigating the murder of your mother. If you continue to derail my investigation, I will drag you down to headquarters and question you there like a common criminal, do I make myself perfectly clear?" snapped Bellamy angrily.

"Forgive me Detective, your eyes are just so piercing. I was getting a little turned on," said Patrice, her voice literally dripping with honey.

"I'm sure we have a female detective I can bring in to finish your questioning," said Bellamy, standing to leave.

"No wait, I promise I'll behave," said Patrice, flashing him a bit of a pout.

Bellamy sat back down and glared at her, he wanted to complete the interview, but he had the sneaky feeling he wasn't going to get a damn thing out of Patrice.

"Really, I want to help," she said, shrugging her shoulders coyly. Bellamy resisted the urge to roll his eyes.

"So, you teach night classes also?" asked Bellamy, he was getting a bit annoyed that he was having to pry everything out of this chick, she seemed to be more interested in flirting with him, than helping out with his investigation.

Her behavior was so abnormal, it was completely throwing him off. For the most part, the family members were either so traumatized by the circumstances they were completely useless, or they talked so much, it was hard to keep them on track. Patrice though, was not easy to figure out. Denning had been right, there was something about the daughter that was not quite right.

"Well no," said Patrice, who's demeanor finally seemed to be changing. Her eyes were cast down and she suddenly couldn't seem to look him in the eye.

"Tell me then, what do you mean you went to class," asked Bellamy, watching her carefully.

"Oh, this is quite embarrassing," she said, wringing her hands nervously.

"Ms. Bernard, I'm not trying to embarrass you, I just need to know your whereabouts since you are the person who was closest to her," said Bellamy.

"I'm taking a salsa class at the community center, I was there till eight. When the class was over, I went out for drinks with a gentleman I met at class," she said, her cheeks were now flushed bright pink with embarrassment.

"Salsa class? You mean, salsa dancing?" asked Bellamy, trying hard to hide the shock in his voice. He couldn't help it, he couldn't really imagine Patrice salsa dancing.

"Yes, salsa dancing," snapped Patrice, keeping her eyes cast down in embarrassment.

"This gentleman you went out with last evening. What is his name?" asked Bellamy, looking up from his notepad.

"Why do you need to know his name?" she snapped, glaring at him in shock.

"Ms. Bernard this is a murder investigation, you live with the victim and she is your mother. We will be interviewing others that were close to her in much the same way. Please do not feel like I am singling you out," said Bellamy, trying to put her at ease.

"It's a shame...I was rather hoping that you would single me out," she said, flashing him a sly smile.

"Ms. Bernard, if you cannot focus your attention in my presence I shall have to bring in a female detective to complete this interview. Do I make myself perfectly clear?" cried Bellamy. He had pretty much reached his limit with Sabine Rousseau's thoroughly screwed up daughter.

"You can pretend you don't want me Detective Bellamy, but I've been watching you, it's hard to miss the way you've been checking me out," said Patrice, smiling smugly.

"I'm a detective, I pay close attention to details and I most certainly was not, checking you out," snapped Bellamy, he could almost feel his own face getting red with embarrassment.

"But you were checking me out Detective Bellamy, I noticed it right away. Most men are afraid to admit it, I guess it's just more socially acceptable to pretend to want those women who are basically just skin encased bones. I mean, what's the fun in that? No curves, nothing to grab onto. Do you know what men secretly love the most about fat girls?" asked Patrice, staring him down boldly.

"Ms. Bernard...please..."

"It's their boobs. I mean to a man, a fat girl is like a sexual theme park, lots of boobs and ass..."

"Ms. Bernard..."

"I know you want me. I mean look at these puppies,"

said Patrice, cupping her own breasts in her hands and staring him down seductively. "They're huge!"

Bellamy stood up abruptly and the wrought iron chair he was sitting in made a dull scraping sound on the stone patio as he leapt up from his seat.

"I have nothing further to say to you Ms. Bernard, I will arrange for you to interview with someone else," said Bellamy, fully intending to retreat into the house and leave Patrice there on the patio.

"Eddie Bower," cried Patrice, as he started to walk away.

"What?" he asked, turning around and staring at her as if she had completely lost her mind.

"The guy I went out with last night, his name was Eddie Bower," said Patrice, giving him a wry smile.

"Eddie Bauer, like the store?" asked Bellamy. He had his doubts, he was suddenly getting the feeling that she was lying, this woman was just messing with him, trying to keep him nearby.

"B–O–W–E–R, same name, different spelling."

"OK, I would like to speak with Mr. Bower, do you happen to have his phone number?" asked Bellamy.

"No, I never asked for his number, I had no reason to call him. Our date didn't go as well as I would have liked, Detective Bellamy. When he asked me out, I was under the impression that he wanted to go out get drinks and talk, but he had more on his mind apparently," said Patrice, flashing him a sly smile.

"He wanted to take you home?" asked Bellamy.

"Of course. I guess I should have expected it. It's a repressed desire a lot of men have, having sex with a sexy, curvy woman," said Patrice.

"Sure," snapped Bellamy, fighting the urge to roll his eyes, he just kept scratching notes on his pad.

"You don't believe me, do you detective?" asked Patrice, moving her body a bit closer to his.

"I didn't say that," said Bellamy, still writing, without looking up at her.

"It happens all the time, most guys just assume I'll be easy. They assume that I'm hard up, that I can't get a guy because I'm fat. When the jerk realized he wasn't getting any, our date was suddenly over," said Patrice, grimacing distastefully.

"What club did you go to?" asked Bellamy.

"The Kokomo Beach Club, it's only a couple of blocks from the Community center," said Patrice.

"After that, did you come straight back here?" asked Bellamy, still writing on his notepad.

"Yeah, the club was pretty dead, there was no one there I was interested in," said Patrice shrugging.

"When you came home that night, did you see your mother? Did you speak to her before you went to bed?"

"Well...my mother didn't like it when I went out on dates. So I had lied to her and told her I was going out with the girls. I was upset when I came home because Eddie had turned out to be such a jerk. I was kind of an emotional mess, I didn't want her to see me like that. I snuck in through the back door and went straight to my room. I didn't want to have to face my mother."

"Why not?" asked Bellamy.

"She would just tell me that no guy would ever want me, because I'm so fat and repulsive. It wasn't until this afternoon, I got home from class and I was looking for her and..." Patrice's voice broke, and she burst into tears.

Bellamy took a deep, shaky breath, he hated dealing with grieving families. What can you really say to someone who has just lost a loved one? It was hard to comfort someone when you knew there was really nothing you could do for them. Nothing you can say or do could ever bring their loved one back.

"How old are you Ms. Rousseau?" he asked.

"I'm twenty four," she whimpered, dabbing her eyes with a tissue. "How old are you?"

Bellamy resisted the urge to roll his eyes and ignored her. "Have you ever had a boyfriend?"

"No, not a real boyfriend. Like I said, my mother didn't want me to date. She worried about me. She said all guys want, is to have sex, get you knocked up, and then they leave you," said Patrice, very earnestly.

"And do you believe that to be true?" asked Bellamy.

"Well yeah, why would my mother make that up? She only cares about my welfare," said Patrice, her face was shocked.

"Maybe what she was saying was just a broad generalization, not all men could be bad...right? I mean, what about your father, he was a good man, right?" asked Bellamy, he was trying to tread carefully.

"My father was a disgusting cad who would mount any woman who would let him," said Patrice, rolling her eyes miserably.

Bellamy frowned, Patrice was deteriorating right before his eyes, he had found the source of her anger and her guarded manor was slipping away.

"What about your older sister? She's married, I guess she found a decent man...right?" Bellamy almost shuddered at Patrice's angry expression. She had a deep rooted hatred toward men, this poor girl had probably been brainwashed her entire life!

"I'm the good daughter. I'm the one who stayed here with my mother, I was her companion after my father died. My sister Paloma is the biggest slut who ever lived! My mother told me I'm the pure one. Paloma may be the beautiful one, but I was the good child. Paloma nearly ruined our family," snapped Patrice.

Bellamy was resisting the urge to call off this entire interview. It was obvious that Patrice was severely damaged. At this point, he was not sure he could believe anything that she said. Her mother had apparently filtered everything that she had heard, probably her entire life, he doubted he could get any useful information out of her.

"Did your mother have any enemies, any recent arguments with anyone?" asked Bellamy.

"Would you like to make a list? My mother may have been famous, but she was enemies with nearly everyone she met. I lived with her because no one else would. She has alienated all our friends and relatives, no one has been to our house in years, at least not since my father passed away," said Patrice.

"Yes, I had heard that your siblings are estranged from the family, tell me about them, start with Paloma, since you've already brought her up," said Bellamy.

Patrice sighed miserably and rolled her eyes, obviously her older sister was a bit of a sore subject for her.

"What can I say about my sister Paloma? Of course, she is beautiful, just like my mother. Like my mother, she was a dancer too, she loved to dance, though she had no aspirations to be a prima ballerina like my mother. Paloma loved to dance on stage and in musicals, but her style was more like Fred Astair and Ginger Rogers, she detested ballet. She says it is because our mother crammed it down her throat when she was just a small child. I don't know...that was way before my time.

It wasn't long before Hollywood agents started noticing Paloma too, she had a few small roles in movies and musicals as a child. Then, when she was in her teens her career pretty much took off. Yep, everybody loved Paloma, she was so beautiful and talented. Of course, then there was the car accident."

"Tell me about the accident," said Bellamy, trying to keep Patrice focused.

"It was years ago, but still a horrible tragedy. I wasn't even born yet, but I have heard the stories, they are quite chilling. Paloma almost died. Of course you probably know, her fiancee the movie star Gerard Renoir was killed in the accident, their car was hit by a drunk driver.

I guess it was weeks before my parents were sure that Paloma wasn't going to die from her injuries. My father was completely heartbroken, he and Paloma had been very close before the accident. He worried about her head injury, he was afraid she would never be normal.

Everyone said her recovery was a miracle, she had so many injuries though, the doctors had told her she would never be the same. Of course with her hip and pelvic injuries it was just a given that she would never be able to dance professionally. She fell into a deep depression, everyone became worried that she might never recover, she seemed so lost. My father was beside himself with grief, he finally sent her to live with some relatives in Europe, in the hope that getting her out of Chicago, would do her a bit of good.

She attended college in England and did well academically, but emotionally, her recovery seemed to have come to a standstill. Our parents worried that she might never live a normal life. They arranged for her to be married to a wealthy British nobleman, Arthur Barrington. He had met her several times at social functions and he had become enamored by her beauty.

Paloma herself, seemed to care less what happened to her, so my parents thought the union would be perfect. My parents just wanted her to be provided for. Unfortunately, she disgraced the entire family by calling off the engagement and running off with a degenerate, French hotelier. My mother was completely crushed," said Patrice, her eyes were vacant, she seemed to be deep in thought.

"Was she in love with this man, the one your parents had her engaged to?" asked Bellamy.

"I told you detective, she was basically a zombie! She was emotionally shut down, she didn't care if she lived or died. Who cares if she loved him? The Earl was filthy rich, he seemed to care for her, what else could she have hoped for at that point? My parents were only trying to do what was best for her and the stupid slut had to go and screw everything up!" cried Patrice, angrily.

"This French hotelier that she ran off with. Was she in love with him?" asked Bellamy, still jotting notes on his notepad.

"Yes..she loved him. In fact, I've been told he was the first man she cared about since her fiancee's death. When she met him, it seemed as if she had finally come out of her depression and was slowly returning to normal. It was unfortunate that she had already been engaged to the Earl. My parents would never allow her to marry Stephan, it would be much too scandalous to break her engagement to the Earl."

"Yes, much better to marry a man you are not in love with, than to disgrace your family," snapped Bellamy, with barely concealed sarcasm. This had all happened, most likely before Patrice was even born, yet she recited it all like she had been there every step of the way. Bellamy was sure she had been force fed this, her mother's version of the story, her entire life.

"Detective, it wasn't as if our family were just any Chicago family. My parents are both Hollywood royalty, I'm sure you realize, a scandal of that magnitude...well, it would be unforgivable."

"So Paloma has been estranged from the family all this time? Your parents never forgave her for the crime of falling in love?" cried Bellamy, scarcely able to believe what he was hearing.

"Detective Bellamy, you are jumping ahead, please let me finish my story," said Patrice, flashing him a seductive smile.

Bellamy sighed miserably, if he wasn't already sure of most of the facts, it would be just that...a story. He wasn't sure Patrice could ever be considered a creditable source. Patrice ignored his slightly frustrated demeanor, smiled coyly and began again.

"Paloma ran off to Marseille with her lover, I guess they planned to elope. Luckily, my family found them before they were married and somehow my mother managed to run him off.

Paloma was heartbroken when they broke up, my mother told Paloma she would fall in love again someday, and of course, she did. She focused on getting her education, she went on to medical school and met her husband Drake while she was in residency, they've been married for twelve years now." said Patrice.

"So your mother actually ran off the man Paloma had fallen in love with? How did that go over with your sister?"

"I can only imagine she was angry, but she bounced back just fine. I think I told you this before, but Paloma was a bit of a slut. She was beautiful, men wanted her. Of course, she was always able to use that to her advantage," said Patrice.

"So is your sister happy now? With her husband Drake?" asked Bellamy.

"I never talk to her, she's always so busy. Paloma is a pediatrician outside of Seattle now, she has two kids. I guess she's happy," said Patrice, shrugging.

"What about your other sibling?" asked Bellamy.

"My brother Paul is sadly, a disappointment to my parents. He was always a bit of a slacker. He went to college, but he was so busy partying he barely squeaked by. While he was still in college, he got his girlfriend pregnant.

He offered her money for an abortion, but her brother showed up the next day and beat the shit out of him.

Of course, my father made sure he did the right thing, he married her and they have two young boys. He lives in Indianapolis, he's an electrician and he has his own company. Of course, daddy gave him the money to start his company, but I believe he's making an honest living now," said Patrice, with a little sigh.

Bellamy was frowning, wondering how much of these stories were true, or what may have been fabricated by her mother. It seemed that when someone did something Sabine didn't like, she held a grudge, and she would embellish the story for Patrice, who was also expected to carry the grudge.

"When was the last time you saw Paloma and Paul?" asked Bellamy.

"I saw them briefly at my dad's funeral, but not since. My mother made a bit of a scene at the funeral," said Patrice, grimacing painfully.

"What sort of a scene?" asked Bellamy, he was almost salivating, finally, he was getting somewhere.

"It was all Paloma's fault, my mother didn't want a funeral, she wanted my father cremated and no ceremony. My dad didn't want people making a fuss over him after he was gone. He wouldn't have wanted it. Paloma insisted that we have some sort of a memorial service, at least for the family, so all us kids could have a little bit of closure.

Paloma and Paul set everything up and my mother was very angry that they had defied her wishes.

My mother wasn't going to go at all, but at the last moment she ended up going. The service was beautiful, the speakers said so many nice things about my father. At the end of the service they played my father's favorite song. It kind of got to me, and I started sobbing. My mother got very upset with me for loosing control of my emotions like that in front of everyone, she never cried in front of anyone, she told me it was a sign of weakness. She got very angry and started screaming at me, telling me I was acting like a child," said Patrice, taking a deep, shaky breath.

"That must have upset you," said Bellamy.

"Yes, it made me cry more. Then she said..." Patrice was suddenly sobbing again, unable to speak.

Bellamy took her hand gently, in a show of support. This woman was having the most trying day of her life. He felt bad for her.

"She said..."

"What did she say Patrice?" he asked.

"She said, I don't know what you're so upset about. He wasn't even your real father!" cried Patrice, sobbing uncontrollably.

Bellamy frowned distastefully and took Patrice into his arms and held her while she sobbed.

Chapter 4

Detective Salazar glanced around the tidy study, trying to visualize what had happened here, sometime this morning.   Denning had been right, it appeared that someone had come for tea and at some point and something had gone horribly wrong.

The spilled tea from one teacup was the only thing in the entire room that suggested a struggle.   That and the dark red, arc of arterial blood splatter on the wall, and the partially congealed bloodstain on the oriental rug, which remained after the body had been removed.

Salazar ambled slowly about the house, looking for anything that might indicate who Ms. Rousseau's last visitor might have been.   A friend, a lover, a delivery man.   So far, he had found absolutely nothing.   The house was obsessively clean, there was barely a clue that anyone lived here, let alone entertained any visitors here.   He walked slowly up the ornate, curving, walnut stairway, carefully observing his surroundings as he ascended to the second floor.   He wanted to check out the bedrooms.

The first room he came to was obviously the master suite.   The room was large and airy with an entire wall of windows.   The king sized bed was neatly made with a painted silk coverlet and the matching draperies were open, flooding the room with light.

The room was clean and elegantly furnished, but to

Salazar it was lifeless, it lacked personality, just like the rest of the house. Salazar walked around the room systematically, snapping photos from all angles. He carefully opened the drawers on the vanity table, but all he found was a host of perfumes and creams that all obviously belonged to Sabine. The room was compulsively clean and offered no clue that anyone had been in the room besides Sabine.

Salazar walked over and opened the doors to the large, walk in closet. It was organized compulsively, much like the rest of the house. The clothing was arranged by color and the shoes were neatly stowed away in boxes that were neatly marked with their contents. He rifled through the hanging clothes and the drawers, but it was obvious all the clothing and the shoes belonged to Sabine, there was not even any evidence that she had ever had a husband.

Salazar ambled into the adjoining bath, it was organized compulsively and spotless as well. Every item in the bedroom and the adjoining bath, obviously belonged to Sabine. Soon Salazar had searched every inch of the bedroom. There was no evidence of a lover, not so much as a stray pubic hair in the bed. It seemed, as if, Ms. Rousseau desired order and cleanliness in her life, above all.

The next bedroom he came to was obviously a guest room. It was the first room Salazar had seen in this house, that wasn't compulsively clean, it was actually a bit dusty. He didn't feel any need to waste his time going through this room, when the CSI's would go through it anyway. He was certain the room hadn't been used in several years. He closed the door carefully and went on to the next room.

He opened the door and his mouth dropped open in shock, he was completely stunned by what he saw inside.

The rest of the house was classically elegant, each piece of furniture and each accessory, was traditional. This room was so out of character with the rest of the house, he wondered if he had stepped into a dream.

Each wall of the large bedroom was painted with elaborate Egyptian murals. The furniture was Egyptian style and there was a large, what appeared to be, mummy coffin, in the corner of the room.

Salazar walked past the large canopy bed which was completely draped in mosquito netting, he was determined to find out what was inside of the coffin. He opened the elaborately decorated coffin slowly, not sure what to expect. He was relieved to see that it was a storage closet for all of Patrice's art supplies, paints, brushes and canvases. He couldn't help but breathe a silent sigh of relief, as he had almost expected to find a second body in there.

His eyes wandered around the large room in awe, unable to believe he was still in the same house. The room had been completely transformed with the murals, the furniture and the decor. Salazar was quite sure that this room belonged to Patrice, though there were no photos or seemingly anything personal in the room.

He headed toward the closet in determination. He flung open the door and was surprised to see a disarray of clothing thrown into the closet. This closet had the same elaborate organization system installed as Sabine's, but much of it was going unused. It seemed to Salazar that Patrice was secretly a slob!

A few items of her plus size clothing had actually made it onto the powder blue, padded hangers, but the bulk of it resided in a large pile in the middle of the closet. Salazar stared in awe, it was the exact opposite of Sabine's neatly organized closet.

He began rooting through the mess of clothing that seemed to be tossed everywhere and there in the back of the closet, were 3 large plastic bins, hidden under all the clothing. He pulled one of the bins out and ripped the top off impatiently. He was surprised to see that it was filled with a variety of junk food. Chips, cookies, snack cakes and soda. He frowned at it distastefully. Obviously, these were the things that Sabine did not allow her daughter to have, but of course, she was having them anyway, in the secret confines of her own room.

Salazar opened all three bins, and found pretty much the same thing in all of them. The daughter, it seemed, had a much different obsession than her mother did. He closed the bins and slid them back into the closet. He looked around the room again in wonder. It was as cold and sterile as the rest of the house, there was nothing personal in this room at all, no photos, no ticket stubs, no notes to self. It was very generically Egyptian.

He walked through all the remaining bedrooms, but much like the first guest bedroom, it was perfectly obvious that no one had used any of the guest bedrooms in the house for quite some time. Salazar walked back down the stairs and checked the remaining rooms on the first floor. He didn't really find anything suspicious, everything was compulsively in it's place and clean. Sabine's murderer had come here specifically to deal with Sabine, there was no evidence of a robbery or that her assailant had been here looking for something.

At that moment, Bellamy walked in through the back door.

"What did you find?" he asked, when he spied Salazar, standing there in the kitchen.

"I found a whole lot of nothin," said Salazar, shrugging his shoulders.

"Did you check the daughter's room?" asked Bellamy.

"Yeah, I checked all the bedrooms, but I didn't find anything relative to the murder. The daughter's bedroom was about as creepy as they come. It was more like the Museum of Natural History, than a twenty four year old woman's bedroom," said Salazar, rolling his eyes.

"Yeah I admit, she is a little weird," said Bellamy, nodding his head.

"A little weird? I get the feeling this chick is freaking

certifiable, you got to go upstairs and see this chick's room. I'm totally serious, she has a freakin coffin up there!" cried Salazar, as Bellamy stared at him dispassionately.

"What else did you find?"

"Well, her and her mother are about as opposite, as opposite can get. Sabine's bedroom is neat and compulsively organized, like the rest of the house. Patrice's room is basically a creepy shrine to the ancient Egyptians, and her closet was a mess, all her clothing laying in a huge pile. At first, I was thinking she was a complete slob, but I'm guessing now that the huge mess in her closet was meant to conceal her huge stash of junk food from her mother, who I am sure, had no clue it was there. My guess is that Patrice must have been deprived of sweets as a child, you should see the stash of junk food she has in her closet, it's freakin unbelievable!," cried Salazar.

"Yeah, from the looks of it, all mommy lets her eat, is salads and grilled chicken. The refrigerator looks like a health food store, no junk food there at all. The fact that she has a secret stash of crap in her room is not really all that surprising to me. I am getting the feeling that Sabine has spent most of her life controlling all three of her children.

I guess the stash of junk food doesn't surprise me too much. I assume it was Patrice's way of rebelling against her mother's overbearing nature. I bet Sabine had no idea why her daughter was so heavy. Sabine's obsession with food apparently fueled a very destructive obsession with food for her daughter," said Bellamy.

"Do you think this chick is damaged enough that she killed her own mother?" asked Salazar.

"She's damaged, there is no doubt in my mind, but there's a lot more in play than we probably realize at this point. I don't want to jump to conclusions, but we definitely can't rule it out yet. I would like to talk to the other two siblings. Momma apparently went coo coo at her husband's funeral. I'm thinking there is a very good reason the other two siblings are estranged," said Bellamy, as he followed Salazar out the front door to their car.

Bellamy slid into the driver's seat and started the car. He glanced up again at the imposing stone mansion. It was definitely the home of a star, and Sabine Rousseau had definitely been a star. He had admired her when he was a child, it seemed strange that she was dead and he would be delving into her personal life, looking for any secrets that might be the key to her untimely death.

Her audience had admired her from afar, but there was someone in her life, possibly someone she had been close to, who had a much lower opinion of her. Maybe it had been Patrice. Bellamy thought about Sabine's unkind words to her own daughter at her father's funeral.

Why would anyone bring her own daughter's world crashing down like that at her father's funeral? Especially, when she was obviously already upset? It seemed cold and calculating, just like a knife to the heart when her daughter was already suffering. Bellamy almost shivered, Sabine had heartlessly injured her own daughter, at a time when she was already grieving.

Was it painful enough for Patrice to actually be a motive for murder? Was it so painful that Patrice, who had already been emotionally damaged by both her parents, felt compelled to cut her own mother's heart out? It was definitely possible...

"I said, does this chick have an alibi?" asked Salazar, jerking Bellamy from his thoughts.

"That's what I want you to check on. She tells me she was at work all day yesterday, then she went to Salsa class last night," said Bellamy.

"Salsa class? That's a scary thought," said Salazar, grinning at him.

"After the class she apparently went out with some guy named Eddie Bower. She claims she never saw her mother that night. She told me she came in the back door and went straight to her room," said Bellamy.

"Eddie Bauer! Shit, why didn't she just tell you she went out with Oscar Meyer, I mean come on, that's a bullshit name if I ever heard one. Did you really believe her? I think she's dicking you around," said Salazar, shaking his head miserably.

"The spelling is different, besides, maybe he was messing with her, or married. I mean think about it, would you tell Patrice your real name? You never know, maybe his real name is Dick Head," said Bellamy, laughing at his own little joke.

"That would be more believable," laughed Salazar.

"Check out the salsa dancing story and check with her work, find out if she's been acting weird lately," said Bellamy.

"I'm getting the feeling her co workers wouldn't know the difference," said Salazar.

"Yeah, well do the best you can. I'm going to talk to the other two siblings, see what they know. Sabine dropped a major bomb on Patrice at her father's funeral and told her that he wasn't her real father. Maybe if Patrice truly is a bastard child, one of them might know who the guy was that fathered her," said Bellamy.

"Good luck with that, it sounds like this family puts the fun in dysfunctional," said Salazar, laughing.

Bellamy turned up the music and blasted the AC, this entire case was disturbing him. He was leaning toward the theory that an emotionally damaged Patrice had murdered her mother and cut out her heart to send the world a message. Right now, he had no evidence to back that up. He knew that he and Salazar had their work cut out for them.

Chapter 5

Bellamy stifled a bored yawn. He was sitting at his desk, stacking up pencils in boredom. He was distractedly stacking them into tiny log cabins. He sighed in frustration and ran his hand through his hair causing it to stick up wildly, like the back of a porcupine. He had never been good at waiting and the minutes seemed to be creeping by at a snail's pace.

He rubbed his eyes wearily. So far, his entire investigation had hit one roadblock after another. His interview with Patrice hadn't been helpful at all and so far, he hadn't been able to get in touch with Paloma or her brother Paul, and he was still anxiously waiting for the official cause of death report.

The phone on his desk jangled loudly and he nearly fell out of his chair, he was so startled by the abrupt ringing.

"Detective Bellamy," he snapped.

"Hello Detective, this is Paloma Webster, I'm returning your call. I understand you're working on my mother's case?" asked the soft female voice on the other end.

"Yes, thank you so much for calling me back," said Bellamy.

"Can you please tell me what happened? I was unable to answer your calls because I was already being harassed by reporters here. Their arrival on my front porch was the only clue I got that anything was wrong. I found out from the reporters that my mother is dead, but that is all I know. I'm afraid I'm completely in the dark here, no one can tell me anything," said Paloma.

"Have you spoke with your sister? She is the one who found your mother," said Bellamy.

"No, I'm ashamed to admit, I haven't spoke with my sister or my mother since my dad's funeral, that was more than two years ago. We had a bit of a falling out. Patrice and my mother broke off all contact with Paul and I," said Paloma, her voice was suddenly broken, emotional.

"I guess the best thing is to just be straight with you," said Bellamy, his voice serious and resigned.

"Yes, I'd appreciate that," said Paloma.

"Your mother was murdered at home in her mansion," said Bellamy, he paused when he heard Paloma gasp in shock. How horrible to be approached by reporters, before you even knew the real story of your mother's death.

"Murdered?" she managed to whimper, when she finally found her voice.

"I'm very sorry Mrs. Webster, I'm heartbroken to learn that the press was able to get to you first," said Bellamy.

"Go on, tell me what happened," said Paloma, forcing her voice to sound strong.

"Patrice found her body in the study this afternoon when she came home from work. Your mother was stabbed multiple times. My best guess is that it was someone who knew her well. The person was apparently there for tea, there were no real signs of a struggle and there was no forced entry into the house," said Bellamy.

"No forced entry?" asked Paloma, her voice seemed to be considering the possibility. "So you think it was someone she invited to the house, like a lover?"

"Possibly. Do you know if your mother currently had a lover?" asked Bellamy, suddenly intrigued.

"Like I said, I haven't spoke with my mother, or Patrice for two years, but I wouldn't be surprised. My mother always kept herself surrounded by men. When she was younger, she was so beautiful, I imagine she could barely keep the men away. When she got older, she had many affairs, I believe to reinforce to herself that she was still attractive. My mother has always been quite vain, she needed constant reassurance about her beauty," said Paloma, thoughtfully.

"How did you feel about your mother having multiple affairs?" asked Bellamy, trying very gently to hit a nerve. He wanted to tap into this daughter's feelings for her mother, without her realizing what he was doing.

"What do you mean, how did I feel about it?" asked Paloma, her voice suddenly suspicious.

"Did the two of you ever fight about her infidelities? Patrice has told me that you were very close to your father. Perhaps her affairs angered you, maybe the two of you fought about them, maybe there was name calling, hurt feelings," suggested Bellamy, really only wanting to get an idea of this sister's mental status. Hopefully, she wasn't as screwed up as Patrice.

"Detective, over the past twenty years I have learned to separate myself from my mother's affairs. I could care less what my mother did anymore. Over the years, I have gotten quite used to her need to be the center of attention. For me, it was just easier to keep my distance from her, I needed to live my own life, without her constant interference," said Paloma, her voice was cold.

"So I take it, the two of you didn't have the best relationship," said Bellamy, gently digging.

"It wasn't for lack of trying on my part. I spent the first twenty years of my life, struggling to earn my mother's approval, never knowing that no matter what I did, I would never be good enough, as far as my mother was concerned."

"So the relationship was strained," said Bellamy.

"Strained would certainly be a nice way of putting it. I was an inconvenience, at best, in my mother's life. My mother had never wanted children. I was really just an unfortunate accident, as far as she was concerned. She loved being a star and she loved being the center of attention, especially where men were concerned. My mother wasn't happy unless everyone in the room was paying attention to her.

Paul and I were nothing but cute little accessories she brought out when she thought we might impress someone.

As far as her infidelity, even as a small child, I realized she was cheating on my father. Whenever Daddy was gone, Paul and I had to be in bed by eight, by eight thirty we could usually hear an unfamiliar male voice in the foyer, and laughing. There was always lots of laughing.

After a few drinks they would retire to my mother's bedroom. Paul and I couldn't help but know what was going on, they were always so loud. After a while, I guess we got used to it, it almost seemed normal.

When I got older I realized he wasn't faithful to her either, but at least, he had the good sense to not carry on in the presence of his children. I did my best to ignore their infidelities, I mean really, I was just a child, what else could I do?"

"So you never confronted your mother about her affairs, you never got in her face and called her a slut?" asked Bellamy, gently prodding.

"As a child I immersed myself in my studies, I was pretty sheltered by my grandparents. I doubt I even knew what a slut was. In my adult years I avoided my mother as much as possible. I avoided arguing with her, it was not worth it, you could never win, she was always right. I realize she talked about me behind my back, in fact, slut is what my mother called me, especially if I dated a man she did not approve of, which was pretty much all of them.

She never got over the fact that I ran away from my engagement to a nobleman and in her eyes, completely disgraced the family. My mother and father both thought that Arthur Barrington was a splendid catch for me, they pretty much arranged the marriage, but as the wedding approached, I panicked. I couldn't go through with it."

"If you weren't in love with him, why did you agree to the engagement in the first place?" asked Bellamy, wondering if she had truly been that depressed, that she didn't even care what happened to her.

"I don't know. I guess it was just another desperate attempt to try and earn my mother's approval. Do you know how much it hurts to have your own mother criticize every single thing you have ever done in your entire life? I just wanted her to love me, to be proud of me...like a normal parent. After the accident, she had convinced me that I was brain damaged, not really capable of making a sound decision. She told me I was damaged, I would probably never fall in love anyway...I should at least consent to marry this man, who so obviously loved me."

"Did you truly believe that? That you would never fall in love again?" asked Bellamy.

"I don't know. I do know I was completely lost. I guess maybe counseling might have helped, but back then, people just didn't run to the shrink for every little thing," said Paloma.

"I wouldn't really consider the tragic death of your fiancee to be considered a "little thing". Did your mother feel it was beneath your family to ask for help like that?"

asked Bellamy.

"There are lots of things my mother considers to be beneath our family, counseling is just one of those things. Looking back at things now, I'm not sure why I ever went along with the engagement in the first place. I was young, naive, and pretty much convinced that life as I knew it, had ended.

My mother can be quite convincing sometimes. I cannot deny it, I have made plenty of mistakes in my life, but this was marriage...it was huge! At first, it just seemed easier to go along with it, I mean, how bad could it be? He was from a good family, I found his personality tolerable, and he wasn't hideous looking.

The major thing was...I wasn't really attracted to him, so I feared that maybe..."

"Maybe what?" asked Bellamy, still gently prodding.

"I know that this sounds petty, but he was a bit of a stuffed shirt, so I was afraid that the sex would be...you know, not fulfilling. I didn't want to live the rest of my life being sexually frustrated, like my mother so obviously was," she sighed miserably, then she went on.

"Arthur traveled a lot, so I imagined when he was away, I would have my own space, so maybe it wouldn't be that bad. Though after the engagement was official...I don't know...it just seemed all wrong. I wanted to back out respectfully, I tried to tell everyone that it was never going to work, but no one would listen to me."

"That must have been overwhelming, to be trapped in a situation like that, where your whole life seems to be out of your control," said Bellamy, hoping to prod her along. He could feel the emotion seeping into her voice.

"It was very overwhelming for me...that's why I had to run away. No one would listen to me, I was drowning in my fears, yet everything kept moving forward. I was being forced into a marriage with a man I did not love. I was panicking!" said Paloma, Bellamy could actually hear the fear in her voice. He had a satisfied smile on his face as Paloma went on, he had cracked the shell she had constructed around her memories, he was in!

"My mother was so disappointed when I called off my engagement to Arthur, she never forgave me. She thought it was completely preposterous, calling off my engagement to a nobleman. I couldn't help it, I was lost. I was only twenty years old, and I was still emotionally broken and I wasn't sure I would ever heal. My heart felt completely empty, how could that possibly be fair to Arthur? For me to marry him, when my only feelings for him were resigned tolerance. I wasn't ready to settle down, let alone commit to a marriage, especially to someone I had no feelings for. Unfortunately, my parents were determined to push me into this marriage regardless of my feelings." said Paloma.

"That's very harsh, did that make you angry?" asked Bellamy.

"Had I been more mature I might have been angry, but

at the time, I was much too scared to be angry. I had suddenly gone into panic mode and I did what I had to do. I ran off with a rich, French playboy. It was hotelier, Stephan Aubiere. We were already friends, I could see that he was attracted to me...and I...I just wanted to get away from London. My mother swore that I did all this just to embarrass her and my entire family. But I didn't, I ran off with Stephan to ruin my own reputation, so Arthur wouldn't want me anymore, that way he would call off the engagement himself. I could not marry Arthur...I did not love him," said Paloma, sighing.

"Did you love Stephan?" asked Bellamy.

"At first I wasn't sure. Of course, I felt more affection for Stephan than Arthur, we were friends, and the two of us had always had a bond. But after the accident, I was confused. I felt like I couldn't trust my own feelings anymore, I had been so traumatized by Gerard's death. After spending a month in France with him though, it was quite obvious that I was falling in love with him. When we announced our engagement I was very much in love with him. He was the first man I allowed myself to love after Gerard's death. My mother never cared how I felt about Stephan, she was determined to destroy our relationship, and she did."

"Were you ever close to your mother?" asked Bellamy.

"Never. When I was a child, my grandparents raised Paul and I there at the mansion. My mother was too busy traveling between Hollywood, New York and Paris. She was doing what she loved, dancing and making movies. She was very sought after, she really didn't have time to be bothered with her children."

"Were there any good times in your childhood with your mother?" asked Bellamy.

"Like I said before, my mother never wanted me, she had told me, multiple times that I was a mistake. I ruined her career. When we were sick it was Nana and Pappy that were there for us. If it had not been for them, I have no doubt she'd have shipped us off to boarding school somewhere."

"What about your father, Patrice told me he adored you," said Bellamy, carefully trying to arouse Paloma's repressed memories that she had so carefully removed from her consciousness.

"Yes, my father Harvey wanted children desperately, he was fourteen years older than my mother and ready to settle down. I am guessing my mother could have gone her entire life without having children, she didn't think children were cute. If anything, she found them annoying.

I really don't know what happened, I imagine my mother hadn't been careful enough and somehow she got pregnant. When she found out she was pregnant with me she was angry, a dancer's body is never the same after childbirth. Of course, Harvey was ecstatic when he found out she was pregnant, my mother on the other hand was horrified, she wanted to get an abortion, but of course, my father would never allow that. She had no choice but to settle down and become a mom. Paul came along two years later, which made my father very happy. My mother though, was done with the motherhood thing, she went back to work.

When I was older and she realized I was cute, and how should I say it...marketable. She had her agent get me parts in movies and musicals. Of course, she thought it was completely adorable that I was a tiny little version of her. The public ate it up as well and my career seemed to be taking off. She enjoyed taking me out, posing for magazine covers with me. It was like a publicity boon for her.

When I was eighteen she had me cast in a movie that was shooting on location in Paris. That was how I met Gerard. The movie was "No Time Lost" and Gerard and I were cast as lovers in the movie. Mother had read the script and accepted the part for me, so I had no idea what I was getting myself into.

Up to this point I had only played child parts, but this was a love story. I had never had a part that involved kissing, let alone the passionate love scenes that came later in the movie. I was embarrassed by the love scenes because I had never even had a boyfriend before, let alone a lover, so I was a little bit lost.

Luckily, Gerard was very patient and kind to me, both on camera, and off. Before I knew it, I had fallen completely head over heels in love with him. As our on camera romance blossomed, so did our real romance. Looking back on it now, I guess it seems like a bit of a whirlwind romance. When shooting had wrapped up in Paris, the two of us couldn't bare to part. I moved into his Hollywood mansion and just 8 months later, Gerard and I were engaged. My mother was very excited that her own daughter had attracted the attention of such a famous movie star.

Gerard and I planned to be married that September, after the premier of the movie we had starred in together, "No Time Lost". He was almost five years older than me, but I adored him. He loved me so much, he couldn't wait for us to be married.

Everything was perfect, just like a fairy tale, till the accident. When I woke up in the hospital, days after the accident and learned that Gerard had died, I wanted to die myself. I didn't think there was any way I could go on in life."

"What did you do?" asked Bellamy, he felt bad to be dredging up these old memories with her, but a person's history could tell you a lot about that person. Tragedy made some people stronger, others were completely destroyed by it.

"After I finally came home from the hospital I was so depressed, my parents couldn't stand to deal with me any more. They sent me away to live with relatives in Europe. They told me that I needed a change of scenery. I really needed much more than that. I was surviving, but part of me had died in the accident. I was no longer the carefree person I had been before the accident.

I guess it was partly my fault, that my life got so out of control. I'd been bobbing along with no particular direction in life. I was merely existing. When my parents arranged my engagement to Arthur, I could think of no reason I shouldn't marry him, so I went along with it. I didn't think it was possible that I could ever fall in love again. Arthur seemed to love me, so I guess I thought that was as good as it was going to get for me. As the wedding grew closer I started panicking. I knew I could never marry Arthur, I did not love him," said Paloma, sniffling.

"Then what happened?" asked Bellamy, completely amazed that Paloma actually seemed to be completely down to earth and normal.

"When I told my mother that I couldn't marry Arthur she was angry, she threatened to disown me. She didn't care that I had no feelings for him. Of course, I stood to inherit one half of my grandfather's estate when my mother died, but I didn't care. I could not be forced into a marriage with someone I had no feelings for," said Paloma, sadly.

"After you ran away with Stephan, did you ever reconcile with your mother?" asked Bellamy.

"Stephan and I were to be married. I wanted to elope, I was so happy, I didn't want any publicity, and I didn't want any interference. I didn't even invite my parents to the wedding, for fear that my mother would throw one of her fits and ruin everything.

My mother has her connections, so I guess I shouldn't have been surprised that she found out somehow, about our upcoming wedding. She called me at Stephan's manor and hinted that she wanted to come to our wedding, but flying wouldn't be a good idea. I asked her if she was ill and she told me that she was pregnant and she needed me to come home to Chicago."

"Wow," said Bellamy.

"Yeah, I know, right? At first I didn't even believe her, my mother tends to be manipulative, she'll say anything to get her own way. I was skeptical, I thought it was all a ploy just to get me to come home. When the phone calls continued, from both her and Daddy, I began to realize that maybe she truly was pregnant. I guess I started to worry about her a little bit.

I didn't want to come back to the states and be sucked back into all the family drama, but my father was so busy with his projects and my mother was so insistent...she told me she wanted me to come home because she was scared. She was forty two and pregnant, she thought she might die during childbirth," said Paloma.

"Did you come home?" asked Bellamy.

"What can I say Detective? I've been a sucker my entire life. Yes, as stupid as it seems, I came home. She is my mother, and of course, I was worried about her. It turned out to be a bigger disaster than I had ever imagined. When I returned to Chicago my mother managed to destroy my relationship with Stephan and instill in me, a very real fear that she would not be a suitable mother for the baby," said Paloma.

"This baby, it was Patrice, am I right?" he asked.

"Yes," said Paloma.

"What did you do?"

"After my relationship with Stephan was destroyed and he returned to France, I became obsessed with the safety of the baby. I feared Patrice would face the same rejection that Paul and I had, and it was my intention to take the baby and make her my own. I offered to adopt her," said Paloma.

"Was your mother agreeable to this?"

"Absolutely not! My mother has always been hateful that way. When she senses someone wants something, it only makes her hold on to it tighter, even if she has no desire to keep it for herself," said Paloma.

"What did you do then?"

"Unfortunately the only thing I could do was take her to court. I couldn't bare the thought of another child facing the same loveless upbringing Paul and I had endured. I thought that everyone would be able to see what I saw when I looked at my mother, but I was wrong. I had underestimated my mother and how hard she would play the game, she has always been an excellent actress. After her award winning performance on the stand, they were convinced that she was a perfect mother and I was her crazy, disgruntled offspring. The court had no choice but let the loving mother keep her precious child and rule against her crazy, slutty, daughter," said Paloma, her voice finally dripping with hatred.

"Your mother really hurt you, didn't she?" asked Bellamy.

"Detective, my own mother has dragged my name through the mud every chance she had, in an effort to make herself look that much more perfect. She has hurt everyone she's ever had contact with, she is the most toxic person I have ever met in my life," sighed Paloma.

"Did you kill your mother Mrs. Webster?" asked Bellamy, just to hear what she would have to say.

"That would be much more trouble than anyone should have to endure, where my mother is concerned. So no, I did not. Though if you don't believe me, you can check with the hospital and my office. They can confirm that I have been here in Seattle, putting in twelve to fourteen hour days," said Paloma.

"What did you mean, when you said it would be too much trouble to murder your mother?" asked Bellamy. He wondered if she was still suffering from depression and just didn't care.

"I mean my mother isn't worth it. I decided a long time ago that she isn't worth even one more minute of my passion or anger. After my father died, I figured she'd die in her own misery soon enough. How can someone so completely miserable continue in life for long? My only regret is that I didn't fight harder to save my sister, or half sister I guess, from a life under her thumb. Had I raised her, maybe Patrice would be normal," said Paloma.

"What do you mean? Normal?" asked Bellamy, hoping to get Paloma's candid opinion on her decidedly screwed up sister.

"Poor Patrice, where do I start? I'm not a psychiatrist, but she has issues. She has been morbidly obese since she was just a small child, she's never had a boyfriend, though I'm not sure if that is because of the obesity, or the fact that my mother has told her repeatedly that I am the family slut," said Paloma, sadly.

"Yes, she did mention that to me," said Bellamy.

"Of course she did. Like I said, I haven't really spoke with her, since the drama at my father's funeral, but she has been in trouble before, apparently related to some inappropriate sexual behavior," said Paloma.

"Hmmm, she didn't mention that, could you be a little more specific?" asked Bellamy, trying to hide the smug smirk in his voice.

"I had heard she was put on probation regarding two separate incidents. She apparently groped a co worker at an off campus function, and she flashed her breasts at student in the college parking lot," said Patrice, distastefully.

"Let me just ask you this. Do you think Patrice was sexually abused as a child?" asked Bellamy. He already knew that Patrice's behavior was not normal, sometimes past sexual abuse was the root of inappropriate sexual behavior.

"That is something I have suspected for quite a few years, since Patrice has always been a bit inappropriate. I've asked her and she has denied it, but it's just that..."

"Please, tell me what you are thinking," said Bellamy.

"Detective, I know my father would not have been capable of such a thing, he loved us, even Patrice. But like I said, my mother always had lovers over to the house, some of them were kind of creepy. I woke up one night to find one peeking in my door, watching me sleep. I never forgot to lock my bedroom door after that night. I always wondered if one of Mother's creepy lovers had maybe got to her," said Paloma, he could almost feel her shudder as she spoke.

Bellamy almost shuddered too, he couldn't imagine living the childhoods that Patrice and Paloma had both endured. He had decided that being poor and happy, was much better than rich and miserable.

"Before your mother announced it at the funeral, did you know that Patrice was not your father's child?" asked Bellamy.

"Not officially, I had my suspicions of course. When Patrice was conceived, my father was working on a movie that was being filmed, mostly in Romania, he had hadn't been home at all, anytime close to Patrice's conception. I never said a word, although I was suspicious. My father never voiced his suspicions, at least, not to Paul or I. In the past, others have mentioned that Paul and I both look a lot like our father, yet Patrice doesn't seem to resemble him at all. My father worked hard to quell all the rumors around Patrice's birth. His own pride would never allow my mother's adulterous nature to come out." said Paloma.

"Of course, that would be embarrassing for your father as well, to admit that his wife had been screwing around on him while he'd been away. I'm not sure why she actually carried the child to term, I mean if it was that obvious that Harvey wasn't the father, why wouldn't she just abort the fetus? I mean you said she had considered abortion with you. Was she trying to anger Harvey?" said Bellamy.

"Call me crazy, but I had always felt my mother had become pregnant on purpose, not to anger my father, but to get me to come home from France. She felt like I was embarrassing the family, running off with a French hotelier and ditching the Earl. She's always been very controlling and for once, I wasn't listening to her. I had fallen in love with Stephan, I was finally happy. But of course, she could care less if I was happy," sighed Paloma, her voice was emotional.

"So you believe she got pregnant on purpose, to play on your feelings?" asked Bellamy, almost wanting to burst out in laughter, the whole idea sounded ridiculous as far as he was concerned.

"Either that or it was a very well timed accident. Like I said, she always knew how to control me, and she knew I would do anything to protect a child from the life that Paul and I had endured. She never had a shortage of lovers, so it would have been quite easy. The fact that my father spent a great many weeks in Romania, made it even easier I'm sure. In fact, I'm not even sure she knew who Patrice's father was.

"So you have no idea who Patrice's father might be?" asked Bellamy, sighing miserably. It seemed like he had just hit another brick wall. Paloma lived in Seattle, he was almost certain, she could not have pulled off her mother's murder.

"I was in France during the time Patrice was conceived, but maybe Paul would remember," said Paloma, though she had serious doubts Paul would remember any of that. Apparently, Paul had also tried his hardest to keep his distance from his harshly judgmental mother.

"Thank you for your time Mrs. Webster, I'll let you know if I get any leads," said Bellamy, bidding her good bye, and staring numbly at the phone after he set it down.

Paloma seemed normal enough, despite the fact that her mother had been extremely overbearing. She had managed to escape her mother's tight grasp and go on to live a normal life, or so it seemed.

Bellamy jumped when suddenly his office door was

flung open and Salazar burst in excitedly.

"Hey, we got to go back and talk to the psycho daughter again, her whole story was a wash," cried Salazar, excitedly.

"Like how?" asked Bellamy, not really convinced.

"I just got done talking to the instructor of the salsa class at the community center. Patrice wasn't even enrolled in the class, she's like a stalker, she just hangs around and watches the class. And get this, there is no Eddie Bauer in the class, but there is a guy named Edwin Sterling that Ms. Bernard has apparently been making eyes at."

"Did you call him? What did he say?" cried Bellamy, excitedly.

"Chill out will ya, I'm getting to that. So anyway, the instructor gave me old Eddie's address and phone number. I called him and told him it was imperative that I meet up with him. He lives in a stuffy little apartment about half a mile from the community center. He's nothing special, he's kind of nerdy and probably a little bit desperate. He has apparently been divorced for about two years, so yeah, he was looking for some action. I mean after more than two years the old guy was getting bored with just flogging the old log," said Salazar, with a laugh.

"Yeah, yeah...so what did this loser say about Patrice?" asked Bellamy, rolling his eyes miserably.

"He admitted he went out for drinks with Patrice, except he didn't ask her out, he told me Patrice asked him out!" cried Salazar.

"Okay, so she embellished the story a little bit," said Bellamy, shrugging.

"A little bit! Listen to this, this guy said she asked him to go out for drinks that evening. He wasn't so sure, there was another hot divorcee at the class he was hoping to put the moves on. Unfortunately for old Eddie, he's shy...too shy to approach the hot divorcee. So Patrice makes the moves on him, he kinda feels sorry for her. You know, she's kind of homely looking, and she told him she's never been with a man before."

"She said that? She's never been with a man before?" asked Bellamy.

"Well according to Eddie, though he wasn't really thinking with his big head. Of course, he can't help considering just doing her, cause he's nerdy and he hasn't got laid since he got divorced more than two years ago."

"Hmmm, so he's shy and horny...I guess Patrice is looking better and better to Mr. Sterling," said Bellamy, stifling a sly smile.

"Yeah right, so anyway, he figures what the heck, he'll go out with her. He figures if nothing else, maybe he'll get lucky. He had no idea what was in store for him. So they have a few drinks and before you know it, she's all hot and bothered and whispering in his ear and he knows she's ripe for the picking.

So they blow the bar scene and as soon as they get to her car, she jumps him and tries to ride him like a stallion, only it don't work out...he can't get it up, cause he's too scared. The poor bastard said he never had a woman attack him like that!" said Salazar laughing, hysterically.

"Yeah, that's weird," said Bellamy.

"Wait, that's not the end of it! So she brings the poor guy back to her place, the friggin Egyptian tomb, and of course he's freaked out by that because face it, it's just friggin creepy. At this point, the guy is having second thoughts about everything and he wants to leave, but she refuses to let him leave till they do it!" cried Salazar, his face flushed with excitement.

"So what happened?"

"So she works on this poor bastard's limp noodle for like an hour, and still he's too scared to get it up, so she pulls out a vibrator, and starts doing herself in front of him, hoping it will get him going. Instead, at this point the guy is so freaked out by this chick, he's pretty much ready to shit his pants. Only she won't let him have his pants! Finally, when she realizes he's never going to get it up, she calls him an impotent bastard and kicks him out of the house, wearing nothing but his t-shirt and his tidy whities," said Salazar, completely amused by his own story.

"Jesus, that's creepy," said Bellamy, shaking his head in disgust.

"I know, right?"

"I guess the poor guy's probably never going back to salsa class, huh?" asked Bellamy, flashing his partner a sly smile.

"You betcha," said Salazar.

"Knock knock," called a voice from outside the door.

"What ya got Penny?" cried Bellamy, standing up and striding toward the door and opening it.

"I've got semen," said Penny, holding a printed report up in front of Doug's face.

"Is that like crabs? Cause crabs are contagious," said Salazar, laughing heartily.

"We found semen in the vaginal vault, knucklehead! Ms. Rousseau had sex sometime before she was murdered," said Penny, smiling proudly.

"Sometime? What kind of time frame are we looking at here?" asked Bellamy, suddenly intrigued.

"Up to several hours before. So I guess we're looking for a lover," said Penny.

"Or a rapist," said Salazar, with a shrug.

"No...I talked to Brad, he's done his exam, there was no evidence of forceable sexual activity, this was obviously consensual sex," said Penny.

"What else?" asked Salazar.

"There is nothing else, no finger prints, no fibers, nothing. Whoever did this was invited into the house as a friend, but they were anything but. They murdered Ms. Rousseau and left without a trace," said Penny.

"No, that's impossible, everyone leaves something behind, I have no doubt we will find it. At least we have semen, that should be helpful," said Bellamy.

"So far no hits in the system though. If it belongs to someone who's not in any of our databases, we might not ever find out who it belongs to," said Penny, shaking her head sadly.

"Why don't you go back to your lab and check some more databases," said Salazar, rolling his eyes at her.

"Bite me," snapped Penny, turning and heading out of the office in a huff. Bellamy almost laughed. He could see there was a little bit of chemistry between Penny and Salazar, but whenever he was around they both pretended to hate each other but unbeknownst to the two of them, he could see exactly what was going on.

"So, you want to go back out and talk to the daughter again?" asked Salazar, giving Bellamy an evil grin.

"You know what? Why don't you talk to her this time? Maybe you'll have better luck with her than I did. I want to try and contact the brother again," said Bellamy.

"Oh no, I ain't going out there by myself. I don't want that chick jumping on me like a dog in heat," cried Salazar, his eyes suddenly as wide as saucers.

"You big pussy, take a uniformed with you if you're too scared to go alone," said Bellamy, with a little laugh.

"Hey, I got enough women who want this, I don't need no broad that outweighs me by about sixty pounds climbing on and riding me like I'm Secretariat," laughed Salazar, flexing his muscles and strutting around like a rooster.

"Hey Chris, I hate to tell you this, but you are no thoroughbred," said Bellamy, shaking his head miserably and laughing.

"Hey you're just jealous cause I can have any woman I want, and you're an old married guy, you been doing the same old lady for what, 18 years!" laughed Salazar.

"No, you're the one who's jealous, because I've been married for 18 years to the hottest chick you've ever seen! Besides, I've been "doing her" for more than twenty years," said Bellamy, giving his partner a little wink.

"You're right, Patty is pretty hot, you lucky bastard," said Salazar.

"Go interview Patrice. Besides, it's your turn, and I have seniority," said Bellamy.

"Yeah, that's the only perk you get for being an old fart," said Salazar, making a face at him before he ducked out the door. Bellamy laughed as his partner ducked out. He was anxious to hear all about Salazar's interview with Patrice.

Chapter 6

Salazar was standing with his arms folded across his chest, staring blankly through the one way glass of the interrogation room. He was watching Patrice squirm uncomfortably on the vinyl chair, he was sure she knew he was watching her. Out of her own environment, her arrogance had melted away and Patrice Bernard was meek and nervous, just like any other suspect.

He had made the decision to bring her here to headquarters in an attempt to level the playing field a little bit. He was a bit nervous about her history, he was pretty sure she was more than a little unstable. He thought it was best to bring her here to headquarters, where he could control the environment a little bit.

Salazar picked up two bottles of water and walked nonchalantly into the room. He stared her down confidently as he approached the long table. Patrice's nervous gaze followed him as he crossed the room and pulled out the chair across from her.

"Why have you brought me here to this godforsaken dungeon of a room? Am I a suspect, are you going to charge me with something, detective?" she snapped, her words were laced with sarcasm.

"Right now everyone is a suspect, and you my dear, are at the very top of our list," said Salazar, flashing her a sly smile.

"Me, why would I be at the top of your list? I'm merely a victim here. I was devastated when I found my mother's body. It is just inconceivable to me that you actually plan on interrogating me more. You should be out there looking for her murderer," she snapped angrily.

"You lived with her, you stand to gain a lot now that your mother is dead. Besides, you weren't completely cooperative or honest with Detective Bellamy," said Salazar.

"How could I be? The way he kept propositioning me and he couldn't take his eyes off of me. It was a bit unnerving," said Patrice, flashing him a coy smile.

"Yes, I imagine it was," said Salazar, carefully concealing the urge to break out in maniacal laughter, this chick was flipping nuts!

"Before we begin, do you have anything you would like to tell me?" he asked, flashing her a bit of a sly smile. She appeared to be unmoved as he handed her one of the water bottles. He was hoping to use his charm to flirt with her a little bit, but she was strangely immune to his charms.

"No," she snapped. She looked away nervously and cracked the water bottle open without looking up at him. Salazar refused to break the stained silence, he wanted her to say something. She glared at him, then she took a long sip of her water. He sighed miserably, she may be crazy, but she wasn't stupid.

"Ms. Bernard, do you know why I brought you here today?" he asked.

"You already told me. For some reason, not entirely clear to me, I am apparently a suspect," said Patrice, rolling her eyes at him and shrugging nonchalantly.

"You have no clue as to why you might possibly be a suspect?" asked Salazar, giving her his most serious look.

"I believe it is entirely because Detective Bellamy wanted to see me again. I think he finds me quite attractive. When he interviewed me at the house, he couldn't stop staring at my boobs," said Patrice, raising her eyebrows at him.

"No, Ms. Bernard..."

"See, that's the power of suggestion, now you can't stop staring at them either. They're not silicone, they're real...you want to feel?" she asked, smiling at him seductively.

"Can you cut the crap please? There's a reason I brought you here today, and it's not cause anybody here wants to feel up your tits. I brought you here today because I talked to your date, "Eddie"," said Salazar, flashing her a slow, easy smile. She gave him a shocked look. He raised his eyebrows at her and stifled a bit of a chuckle...game on bitch, he thought.

Patrice just sat there glaring at him silently. He almost lost his cool and laughed, he was proud of himself, he had actually rendered her silent.

"Hmmm, I get the feeling you had no idea I would actually talk to Eddie, who's name happens to be Sterling, not Bower. Now tell me Ms. Bernard, would you like to change your story?" he asked, raising his eyebrows at her.

"You have no right to pry into my personal life like this, what I do with my personal time is no concern of yours!" she shouted angrily, her face suddenly red.

"I have every right, this is a murder investigation and believe you me, I will be checking out even the tiniest details. Your mother was murdered in your house, and you found the body. I would appreciate your full cooperation, don't make me take you into police custody," snapped Salazar.

Patrice sighed miserably. "Okay, I lied. I'm sorry, I was embarrassed. Would you want to tell someone, you are so repulsive to men, you pretty much have to rape a guy, to get him to have sex with you?" asked Patrice.

"Ms. Bernard this is very serious, if you know what is good for you, you will be completely honest with me. Right now you are the primary suspect in a murder investigation. We are talking about your alibi here, I need you to be straight with me," said Salazar, staring her down intently.

"What exactly, makes me the primary suspect? Lack of a better choice?" asked Patrice, shaking her head, miserably.

"Motive, opportunity, and the fact that you have already lied to Detective Bellamy. What else have you concealed from us?" asked Salazar, giving her a cool glare.

"I'm sorry Detective Salazar, no more lies," said Patrice, shaking her head resolutely.

"Fine, I want you to tell me what really happened that night, no more lies, no omissions, no embellishments, am I clear?" asked Salazar, eyeing her unemotionally.

"Yes, perfectly clear. OK, so I went to watch the salsa class that night, my friend Alyce was taking lessons and she had told me about Eddie," said Patrice, rolling her eyes miserably.

"She told you what about Eddie?" asked Salazar.

"She told me that Eddie was taking lessons and she was pretty sure he was only there because he was on the prowl for a woman. Alyce told me he was divorced and lonely. He wasn't much to look at. I mean, he was just a mousy looking, balding guy, so I figured it would be easy. I mean, obviously being divorced, he wasn't getting any. He seemed receptive enough when I asked him out."

"After we had drinks I was a little buzzed and horny, I made the moves on him in the car in the parking lot. He was having a little bit of trouble...umm, getting it up. He told me he needed complete privacy, because he was nervous. At that point I was so horny, I was determined to get laid...whenever, however, so I took him back to the house," said Patrice.

"To your room?" asked Salazar.

"Of course, where else would I take him?" asked Patrice, seemingly annoyed.

"Did your mother see the two of you together?"

"No," snapped Patrice.

"Are you quite certain? I get the feeling she was very protective of her little girl," said Salazar, flashing her a sly smile.

"Of course, she could screw whoever she wanted to, but I was condemned to live my life like a nun, she didn't want me to ever meet a man," said Patrice, rolling her eyes distastefully.

"Did she forbid you to date?" asked Salazar.

"She didn't forbid me, per se. She tried to scare me...she told me the men would use my body for sex and then throw me away. She told me I was lucky I wasn't beautiful like my sister, men wouldn't just see me as an object. At this point in my life I could care less if men used me for sex...it's better than dying a virgin," said Patrice, shaking her head miserably.

"Are you a virgin?" asked Salazar, determined to find out if there were other lovers in the picture.

"I got laid a couple times in college, nothing special. One guy could have been Frankenstein's twin brother. The other guy was totally hot...I'm not really sure why he hooked up with me. It was at a Frat party. I was totally wasted. I think it may have been a dare, for his Frat initiation. Some guys will do anything to get into the right Frat."

"No recent lovers?" asked Salazar.

"No, unfortunately I am not completely gorgeous like my sister. She spent the better part of her twenties fending off men. I'm sure she could have had whoever she wanted," said Patrice, frowning.

"You hate that, don't you? Your mother has always hated that, hasn't she? That your sister was beautiful and men were drawn to her. I bet it angered your mother that Paloma was able to attract a famous movie star like Gerard Renoir. Then to be engaged to nobility and throw it away like that..." said Salazar, trying to cautiously open up some old wounds for Patrice.

"Mother was furious about the fiasco with the Earl, it was bad publicity for the family for months. My brother Paul forgave her for making a mockery of our family. He said it wasn't her fault, after the accident she was lost. Gerard had been the love of her life, she could barely function after she found out he was gone. It was only later that she went away to Europe, but she still wasn't herself, she was out of control," Patrice's eyes were vacant. She had lapsed back in time, her opinions were no longer her own...they were her mother's.

"Maybe she didn't do it to make a mockery of your family. Maybe your family was trying to control her and she didn't want to be controlled. Maybe she wanted to make her own decisions," said Salazar, giving her a sly smile.

"My parents only wanted her to have the best things in life. Paloma wanted love, but what is love anyway, but a useless, fickle emotion?" snapped Patrice, her face was flushed again and she seemed to be fighting anger.

"What about your mother? She wasn't perfect, she had affairs, right? I mean, she did announce at your father's funeral that you weren't even his child...that had to hurt," said Salazar, swallowing anxiously. He was well aware his most recent question might very well push Patrice right over the edge.

"It was a lie! She was hurting and she meant to hurt me! My parents were married for forty five years, they were never unfaithful to each other!" cried Patrice, standing abruptly and staring the detective down, her eyes shining with malice.

"Paloma certainly wasn't surprised by your mother's confession. In fact, your mother had so many affairs, Paloma couldn't even take a guess at who your true father might be," said Salazar, subconsciously bracing himself for the storm.

"Paloma is a fucking lying bitch! That little whore was so busy fucking every guy in Europe, she had no idea what was going on here!" cried Patrice, now thoroughly enraged.

"So your mother never had any affairs, to your knowledge," said Salazar.

"No, my mother was a star, a dignified woman, she would never sleep around. My sister was a terrible embarrassment to the family, my parents were happy she finally found a guy to marry her, so she would settle down," said Patrice, who was also slowly settling down.

"Let's go back to Mr. Sterling. You brought him back to your room, did the two of you have intercourse?" asked Salazar.

"Yes," said Patrice, eyeing him arrogantly.

"So he managed to overcome his initial stage fright, and perform," asked Salazar, eyeing her carefully.

"Yes," snapped Patrice.

Salazar resisted the urge to roll his eyes. "Afterwards, did he leave, or did he stay all night?"

"He left, which was fine with me, he didn't really get me off," said Patrice, raising her eyebrows seductively at the detective.

"Do you think he left right away, or could he possibly have encountered your mother on his way out?"

"I kicked him out, I heard his car pulling away only moments later. There were no other sounds around the house. I assumed that my mother was already asleep," said Patrice, eyeing him calmly.

"The medical examiner found semen in your mother's vagina when he did his exam. Is there any name you might be able to tell me, that might be responsible?" asked Salazar.

"No, I can't say that she ever had any male visitors," said Patrice, staring him down arrogantly.

"Are there others? Perhaps staff who have keys, codes, or other unlimited access to the house?" asked Salazar.

"There's no keys, but there is a keypad at the back door, everyone has their own code, if a member of the staff had come through that door it would be recorded," said Patrice, with a shrug.

"And how would I get such a recording?" asked Salazar.

"The security company could get that for you," said Patrice.

"Well right now, the only man we can actually place at the scene is Mr. Sterling, that makes you a prime suspect, since you were the one who brought him into the house. Maybe he wasn't even a lover, maybe you hired him, maybe he was a hit man. I mean who's to say that you didn't make a little deal with Mr. Sterling and ask him to murder your mother. I mean you do stand to inherit a large chunk of your mother's estate, possibly all of it, since your brother and sister are both estranged from your mother...I mean..."

"I loved my mother, I would never have her murdered!" cried Patrice, suddenly panicking.

"Your mother didn't want you to grow up, she wanted to keep you here forever, under her thumb. Maybe you were jealous of your mother, maybe Edwin wanted her...not you," said Salazar, gently prodding her with his words.

"You sick bastard, are you saying Edwin and my mother had sex?" cried Patrice.

"Can you think of any other man who might have had access to your mother, or your house?" asked Salazar, eyeing her calmly.

"No," said Patrice, eyeing him calmly.

"Then we will have to place Mr. Sterling in police custody, until we rule him out as a suspect. You know, test his DNA, there will be more interrogations, of course. We will need to test your bed linens, of course, we would find a trace of Eddie's semen in your bed," said Salazar.

"No, Eddie didn't do it! He was already gone. You have to believe me!" cried Patrice, her face suddenly consumed with panic.

"We have no choice Ms. Bernard, so far we haven't been able to locate your mother's cell phone, we have no other leads. Sterling is truly the only man we can link to your mother. Now maybe if we knew some of her contacts...you know, like her personal trainer, or other people you may not be familiar with..."

"Wait, here's my mother's blackberry. It has all her contacts on it," said Patrice, pulling it out of her purse and handing it to Detective Salazar.

"Thank you," he said, taking it from her cautiously. He struggled to hide the satisfied smile that threatened to remove the emotionless look, he had on his face. It was hard to remain emotionless, when you've just been handed the piece of evidence that may prove to be the biggest break you've had in a case.

They had looked all over for Sabine's cell phone, without avail. It would be a wealth of information. It would tell him who Sabine had called, who had called her, who her contacts were. Salazar was nearly salivating in anticipation.

"I have a confession to make," said Patrice, staring down at the fake wood laminate of the conference table.

"Yes?" asked Salazar.

"Sterling had nothing to do with any of this. I dragged him back to my house, I just wanted him to want me, but he was impotent, we never actually had sex. I got angry and threw him out of the house, without his clothes..."

"Patrice, I'm very disappointed in you, I trusted you. You told me no more lies," said Salazar, flashing her another, slightly seductive smile.

"I'm sorry Detective Salazar, I will never lie to you again."

JEAN MARIE STANBERRY

Chapter 7

Bellamy was leaning back in his chair, carefully assessing a discolored ceiling tile. It seemed that staring at the filthy shades of rust, brown and tan, was more comforting than thinking about his investigation, which seemed to be going nowhere at the moment.

He had just got off the phone with Sabine's son, Paul. Paul, like his sister Patrice, was obviously just another unfortunate product of an extremely overbearing mother who imagined that the entire world revolved around her. Paul's memories of his childhood ranged from being dragged to publicity photo shoots, where the entire family smiled for the cameras and pretended to be the happy family. To being locked in his room for hours on end, when his father was away and his mother had a lover over. Bellamy's heart grew heavier with each story.

It was sad, Paul hadn't seemed all that shocked or upset when Bellamy told him that his mother had been brutally murdered. Though Bellamy was realizing sadly that this woman, who had been so adored on stage and film, was pretty much hated by those who knew her best.

After spending more than an hour with Paul for on the phone, it had become quite clear to Bellamy that Paul had suffered from years of subtle mental abuse by his mother also. Like Patrice, he had a mostly flat affect and he never offered any information freely, you needed to pry everything out of him.

The strangest thing was, it seemed like his opinions on things could change at the drop of the hat. Bellamy suspected that Paul's own mind was at war within his head. Paul knew what was true and right, but he also knew the answers that his mother coached him to give over the many years. Sabine was gone, but Paul was still anticipating his punishment for saying the wrong thing.

It was becoming quite clear that Sabine wanted her life to have the illusion of order, even if just below the surface everything was falling apart. Bellamy was getting the feeling that in reality, both Sabine and her husband had multiple affairs during their marriage. To everyone on the outside though, they had been true to each other only, it was all merely an illusion.

Poor Paul was so damaged, he could contradict himself in the space of one sentence. It was as if he wasn't sure what was true and what was false, the lies had been told so many times over the years, they almost seemed like fact to him.

Bellamy sighed, no one in this family was going to be of any help to him, they would have to follow what little evidence they had in this case. He picked up the phone and called Penny in the lab to see if she had any new information. He was pleased when she told him she was on her way up anyway, with a new development. In moments she had appeared in his office doorway.

"Hey Penny, did you ever get any hits on that semen in the Rousseau case?" he asked, when he saw her standing there.

"Nothing on the DNA so far, but I did find something else you might find interesting. I've done the microscopic exam on the semen and it was positive for latex and ice crystals," said Penny.

"Ice crystals, what the hell?" cried Bellamy, how could there possibly be ice crystals in the semen?

"Here's my guess, but don't laugh, it may sound a little far fetched. You know me, I do watch a lot of movies, so I have quite an imagination. I believe that someone was set up. I still don't know who's semen it is, but I believe that someone froze the semen from a discarded condom so they could use it to frame that person for Sabine's murder," said Penny.

"Interesting, and not really all that far fetched, as far as this dysfunctional family is concerned," said Bellamy, the gears in his mind were already turning, as he considered that possibility.

"I know," said Penny.

"Hmmm, there was no evidence of rape, but the CSI's did feel that her panties had been pulled up in a way that was not natural. If someone were to use frozen sperm, to implicate someone else, how would they get the sperm in her?" asked Bellamy.

"It's just like artificial insemination, a large, needle less syringe or maybe even a turkey baster," said Penny.

"Hmmm, mumbled Bellamy, stroking his chin thoughtfully. How long would the semen be viable, frozen like that?"

"Well, stored in your normal home freezer, the sperm probably wouldn't be viable for impregnating someone, but the DNA could remain intact indefinitely I imagine," said Penny.

"So theoretically, this could have been sitting in someone's freezer for a very long time," said Bellamy.

"Yeah, theoretically," said Penny, with a shrug.

"Do you know, did the CSI's find anything like that at the scene, a discarded condom in the trash, possibly?" asked Bellamy.

"Nope, whomever did this, cleaned up. The perp was probably as OCD as Sabine herself," said Penny.

"Well that rules out Patrice, compared to her mother, she is a complete slob."

"What about Sabine's other two children?" asked Penny.

"One lives in Seattle, the other in Indianapolis, I seriously doubt either of them made a special trip here to kill their mother, it seems like both of them would rather just keep their distance from her," said Bellamy with a shrug.

The door whipped open and Salazar strutted in with an

excited smile.

"Look what I got," he said, holding up the blackberry in front of them.

"Your phone is beautiful, congratulations," said Penny, rolling her eyes miserably and heading toward the door.

"No, it's not mine, it's Sabine's," said Salazar, giving her a smug smile.

"You're kidding, the CSI's looked everywhere for that thing, how did you get it?" cried Penny, excitedly.

"Patrice had snatched it, she had it in her purse. What do you think about that?" asked Salazar.

"I think the crazy bitch has been lying to us, and I'm getting a little sick of her juvenile pranks. This is a murder investigation, not high school home room!" cried Bellamy, shaking his head angrily. "She told everyone she had no idea what had happened to her mother's phone, I assumed that possibly the killer had taken it. How did you make her give it up?"

"I may not be as experienced as you, but I know women," said Salazar, flashing Penny a seductive smile. "I started pointing fingers at her little boyfriend, I told her we would have to take him into custody and she totally freaked out!"

"Sterling?" cried Bellamy, completely unable to believe it.

"Yeah, she handed this blackberry over so fast, you would have thought it was a hot potato," said Salazar, grinning broadly.

"I think we need to get Sterling in here for another interview, something is up with that guy, and I want to know what it is," said Bellamy.

Chapter 8

Edwin Sterling was squirming uneasily in his chair in the stark white interrogation room at police headquarters. Bellamy and Salazar were both watching him carefully through the one way glass. He'd been in there just over half an hour already, marinating, as they liked to call it. It was a bit of a psychological game, the longer a suspect had to wait for their interrogation, the harder it was for them to keep up with their lies. Sterling's cool was fading fast, he looked as nervous as a rabbit surrounded by coyotes. Finally, Bellamy decided it was time to go in.

"Good morning Mr. Sterling, my name is detective Bellamy, and I assume you already know Detective Salazar, since the two of you spoke previously," said Bellamy, shaking the man's clammy hand, as he stood up nervously when they walked into the room.

Bellamy struggled to stifle a smile, this poor guy was ready to piss his pants he was so nervous, he'd probably never had so much as a parking ticket his entire life. Their plan had been to intimidate him a bit, just to make sure he wouldn't spare any details when he told his story.

Bellamy was wearing a dark, charcoal colored suit and a navy blue, paisley tie. He looked like the classic, Hollywood version of a detective.

Salazar on the other hand, was dressed to enhance his bulk. He was wearing tactical pants, boots, and a tight, black tee shirt that caused his olive skinned biceps to bulge out in all their glory, advertising to everyone that he was not a man to be messed with.

"Yes," said the man, his entire body was stiffened with anxiety.

"Please, have a seat," said Bellamy, indicating that Sterling should sit back down. He fought the urge to offer the man a brown paper bag to breathe into. The poor, clueless bastard looked like he was about to hyperventilate and pass out.

The man slid nervously back into his chair. Bellamy looked him over carefully, the poor guy was so nervous, he was about to come completely unglued. Bellamy knew it wasn't necessarily because he was guilty, some people were just intimidated by authority of any type, especially police officers. This man seemed mild mannered and shy, he had probably been like that his entire life and he had most likely never been in trouble of any sort.

Edwin Sterling was not much to look at. He was probably in his mid forties, though he looked a bit older and he was almost completely bald. He was thin, but not really what anyone would consider fit. He was wearing a blue oxford shirt and khakis, probably stuff he'd had in his closet since the 80's thought Bellamy, as he looked the guy over. He was nervously clearing his throat and he wouldn't make eye contact with Bellamy or Salazar. Bellamy could see why Patrice felt she might have a chance with this guy, he was hardly a prize.

"So Mr. Sterling, due to some recent developments in the case, we have some more questions to ask you," said Bellamy, eyeing him calmly.

"Should I have brought a lawyer?" asked Sterling, his anxiety was almost palpable, a slight sheen of perspiration was appearing on his forehead.

"Do you need a lawyer?" asked Salazar, eyeing him arrogantly.

"I've done nothing wrong," said Sterling, his expression seemed to be softening a little bit.

"Then you have nothing to worry about, we're only looking for answers," said Bellamy.

"What makes you think I would have the answers you are looking for?" asked Sterling.

"You were there in the Rousseau mansion the night before Sabine was murdered. Besides, the story Patrice is telling us and the story you've already told us are not really gelling, we were wondering if you would like to change your story?" asked Salazar, flashing him a self assured grin.

"I told you the truth! Patrice is crazy, there is nothing between us. Yes, I went out with her, I felt sorry for her, but that was a mistake. I just want to forget about that evening, it's like my worst nightmare!" cried Sterling, taking a handkerchief out of his pocket and nervously dabbing his forehead with it.

"I want you to tell me everything, from the time you met Patrice, till the time you walked out the door of her house, do you understand?" asked Bellamy, his voice raising in impatience.

"Yes," said Sterling, swallowing nervously.

"Now tell me, how and when, did you first meet Patrice?" asked Bellamy.

"It was a couple of weeks ago. I don't get out much, so a co worker suggested that I start taking these salsa dancing classes down at the community center. He told me it was a great way to meet women. There's only three guys in the class, but there are thirteen women, most of them are there for the sole purpose of meeting men...and they're desperate. I'm divorced and lonely, it seemed like a perfect idea to me. I'm a financial analyst, so I don't have a chance to meet many women. There were a couple of women at the class I was interested in, but I'm pretty shy, so far I haven't had the nerve to ask any of them out.

Not long ago, Patrice started showing up, just to watch the classes. I can't really dance, so I'm a bit like the comic relief in the class. You know, I'm kind of the nerdy white guy with no rhythm. When Patrice started showing up, she was always staring at me, laughing when I goofed up. I wasn't really attracted to her, but she was always smiling at me. She seemed nice enough, so when she asked me out, I thought, what the hell?

Maybe I just felt sorry for her...I don't know. It's just that she's really heavy and...I'm just not into...I mean, I realize I'm not perfect, and I can handle a little junk in the trunk, but I'm not really into fat girls. I just thought it would be nice to have a friend," said Sterling, giving the detectives a little shrug.

"Patrice didn't want a friend though, did she?" asked Bellamy.

"No," said Sterling, shaking his head miserably.

"At first, things were going fine. When we talked after class, she seemed normal enough. It was later, when she started feeling the alcohol, that things started to deteriorate. We were on our second round of drinks and she started flirting with me, putting her hand on my thigh, whispering suggestive comments in my ear. It's been a long time since I have been with a woman, so I was seriously considering just going for it, I mean sex is sex...right?"

"I imagine," said Salazar, frowning distastefully.

"I guess you've never had that problem, not being able to get laid. Well take my word for it, it sucks. I mean I'm a man, I have needs. Anyway, at that point I had pretty much given in. I mean, I was telling myself since she wanted me so bad, why fight it? Besides, by that point she'd been touching me, I was ready to go..."

"Then what happened Mr. Sterling?" asked Salazar, gently trying to move him along.

"I had already decided I was going to go for it, I mean who says my mind has to realize I'm with a crazy, fat chick. I can fantasize I'm with anyone...right? I was ready to blow the bar scene and give her what she seemed to want so badly, but she ordered more drinks...that's when she started getting angry," said Sterling, with a cringe.

"She was angry with you?"

"No...her mother," said Sterling, shaking his head in confusion and shrugging.

"What did she say?"

"I hadn't realized that her mother was Sabine Rousseau, until she brought it up. I was a bit intrigued, I love old movies, so I have always been a fan of Sabine's. I knew she lived nearby, I started thinking how cool it would be to tell my friends I banged Sabine Rousseau's daughter."

"Really...that's all you could think about, telling your friends?" cried Bellamy, thoroughly disgusted. Salazar snorted in an attempt to hide his laughter, Bellamy gave him a look.

"I wasn't going to tell my friends that her daughter looked like a contestant on a weight loss reality show," said Sterling, shaking his head miserably. "Anyway, as soon as I mentioned I was a fan of her mother's, she started loosing her mind!"

"What do you mean?" asked Salazar.

"Well, she started raising her voice and ranting that everyone loved her mother, everyone thought her mother was so beautiful, but they didn't really know her. If they actually knew her they would hate her," he said.

"Then what?" asked Salazar.

"I was afraid that I had ruined my chances by hitting a raw nerve like that, but in moments her demeanor had changed again. It was as if her outburst of anger seemed to turn her on and she started making the moves on me again," said Sterling, looking a bit embarrassed.

"I know this is a bit personal, but I need details, I need to know her frame of mind that night," said Bellamy, looking at him seriously.

"Her frame of mind was just plain crazy. She started touching me, massaging my crotch, right there at the table, and she was whispering in my ear that she wanted to "suck my cock". I haven't got laid in more than two years, so of course, I couldn't help but respond to her touch. As soon as she could tell I was...ummm, responding to her, she paid the check and we left," said Sterling, blushing in acute embarrassment.

"Where did you go?" asked Salzar.

"We went to her car, we had barely made it inside and she had my pants unzipped. Before I knew it, she was doing all those things she had whispered, right there in the car. There was lots of traffic in the parking lot, car headlights and lots of people walking past. I was having a little difficulty, because the location was so public, but she was adamant," said Sterling, who looked like he was about to pass out, he was so embarrassed.

"Adamant about what?" asked Bellamy.

"That was the embarrassing part, she was so loud! She was shouting at me, screaming that she wanted it, but I was so scared all of a sudden, my erection had all but left. She had climbed on top of me, right there in the front seat of the car, she was trying to stuff my limp dick into her vagina, but of course, it wouldn't work," said Sterling, his face was bright red, his labored breaths had deteriorated to a high pitched wheeze. Finally, he took out an inhaler and took a few puffs.

"I'm very sorry Mr. Sterling. Are you able to go on, or do you need a moment," said Bellamy, feeling bad for the man.

"I'd rather not have this conversation at all," said Sterling, flashing them a rueful glance.

"Hey you play, you got to pay," said Salazar, flashing him a sly smile. "What did the skank do next?"

"She got really mad and started calling me all kinds of hurtful names. As if that was going to make the situation any better. If I could have had a little privacy and a little bit more of that dirty talk I would have been fine, but her demeanor was freaking me out. I couldn't help it, I get nervous sometimes anyway and she was really scaring me, her facial expression alone..." he shivered a little bit, as he recalled the incident.

"What kind of hurtful names?" asked Salazar.

"Well you'd never know it, as sweet as she pretends to be, but she's got a mouth on her. There were so many obscene names, I barely remember. I was trying to tune her out, I was feeling bad enough anyway, the first time in years I get a woman that wants me, and my pecker shrivels away to nothing.

I do know she called me a limp dicked little weasel, that one almost made me laugh, since I'd had a raging hard on, until she went all freaky on me. Finally, I decided I was done with her, I got mad and started to walk back into the bar, I couldn't take the abuse any more. There are plenty of women at the community center that are so desperate, they'll fuck anything with a penis. I was prepared to call a cab and just go home. I was done with Patrice."

"Then what happened?" asked Salazar, this story was so wacky, he was actually almost enjoying it.

"She came after me and apologized. She told me she was mad at me because she thought the reason I couldn't get it up, was because I thought she was fat and disgusting. I told her that wasn't the case at all, I was just embarrassed, the parking lot was so public. She seemed happy with my explanation and started sweet talking me and caressing me again, so of course, I got a little excited. She was pretty pleased, she told me I should come back to her place. Like I told you before, I haven't got laid since my divorce, more than two years ago, so I guess I was thinking with my little head, not the big one. I knew the chick was just plain wacko, but she wanted me so bad, I thought, what the heck? She was the one pursuing me, so I got back in the car and went with her," said Sterling.

"That's when she took you back to the mansion, right?" asked Salazar.

"Yeah, I hadn't been prepared for that, I had assumed that she had her own apartment or something. I wasn't prepared to end up at Sabine Rousseau's mansion," said Sterling.

"What happened next?" asked Salazar.

"I was in awe of the mansion and the fact that it belonged to Sabine Rousseau. I love music and dance and have always been a fan of hers, but my admiration of Sabine seemed to anger her daughter, so I just kept quiet."

"Patrice didn't waste any time, she took me up to her room. I wasn't prepared for that, at all. When I walked in, I thought I was on one of those reality TV shows, you know, the ones where they play a joke on some poor, naive, bastard like me."

"I guess I was in shock, I have never seen anything like it. It looked like a shrine to the ancient Egyptians, not to mention the fact that she had an actual coffin in there," said Sterling, grimacing distastefully.

"Kind of creepy, huh?" said Bellamy.

"Very creepy. I was subconsciously starting to have second thoughts about actually going with her. I was looking around for hidden cameras and I couldn't help but wonder if someone was going to jump out of that coffin and try to scare me.

Patrice was different too, as soon as we arrived in her room her entire demeanor changed again and she was suddenly overbearing and strangely removed, it was as if another personality was emerging. She pretty much threw me onto the bed and started trying to pleasure me again,"

"She was giving you oral sex?" asked Salazar.

"Yes," said Sterling, blushing in embarrassment. "Except there was nothing pleasurable about it. Either she had no clue what she was doing, or she mistakenly thinks that men desire to have their penis pretty much ripped off at the shaft. She was being so rough, she was hurting me, I couldn't really escape, she was on top of me. I mean, she obviously weighs more than me, and there were teeth involved, I was afraid to move. I just wanted to get out of there with my penis intact, I thought she might rip it right off, she was totally freaking me out."

Bellamy had to stifle a laugh, this poor guy looked so embarrassed, he had obviously been traumatized by the whole ordeal. "Do go on Mr. Sterling."

"Well...she was being so rough, it wasn't sensual at all. I was so scared, once again, she couldn't get me hard, which only pissed her off more. She started screaming at me, telling me I was a man, I had a dick, so I should give it to her. I was worried if Sabine was home, she would hear all the commotion and come in there and see us," said Sterling, cringing.

"Did she?" asked Bellamy, almost sure now, that Sabine had come in and seen them together, at this point, it almost seemed as if Patrice had planned it that way.

"Yes," said Sterling, cringing miserably.

"Tell me what happened," said Bellamy, assessing him calmly.

"Well Patrice was still shouting obscenities and carrying on, some of it was so bad, I don't think I can repeat it," he said, distastefully.

"It's okay, we're getting the picture," said Salazar.

"I heard her mother call to her, from outside the door and ask what was going on in there, she sounded angry. If I would have had a boner, I would have lost it at that moment anyway, but of course, I could only think about escaping from that hell, there was no way I could get an erection at that point."

"Patrice yelled to her mother to go away. She yelled at her mother that she had brought home a man and he's fucking her right now. I was shocked, I couldn't believe anyone would talk that way to their own mother. Then she hikes up her skirt and climbs on top of me and starts pumping away like we are having sex. Her mother yanks the door open and walks right in. All I can do is lay there, I can't move, since Patrice has me pinned down. Meanwhile, Patrice pretends to have the most satisfying orgasm ever!" cried Sterling, who was now completely overcome with embarrassment.

"So you believe she wanted her mother to see the two of you having sex?" asked Salazar.

"It was just so dramatic, and of course, I wasn't even really inside of her. It was all just an act. I would have been quite proud of myself, had we actually been doing it, she is definitely the most skilled actress I have ever met. I was probably beet red, since Sabine is standing right there, during all of this carrying on." said Sterling, blushing furiously.

"So Patrice obviously faked an orgasm, all for her mother's benefit. What did you do?" asked Salazar, trying hard to conceal his amusement.

"I couldn't do anything, I was trapped under a woman who probably weighs more than two hundred and fifty pounds, I could barely breathe! After her fake orgasm was over, Patrice acts all shocked and embarrassed that her mother has caught her in the act.

Sabine just gives her a death stare as Patrice is still on top of me, pretending to be completely spent from our act. Sabine just stands there for a few moments, glaring at us. It was the longest strained silence I have ever endured. Sabine looked so angry, I almost expected her to come over and beat the crap out of me for screwing her daughter. Anyway, Sabine called Patrice a stupid whore and then she walked out," said Sterling.

Bellamy had to bite his lower lip to avoid laughing, this

poor guy was so horrified by his entire ordeal, and he couldn't blame him, what a nightmare! "Please go on Mr. Sterling."

"Patrice was so satisfied by her mother's behavior it was almost as if she really did have an orgasm. She was completely ecstatic! I was ready to grab my pants and leave, I was so shook up, but she became determined again, to truly have sex with me.

What she didn't realize was I was so freaked out, I thought I might never get another boner again...ever! I just wanted to escape, she was completely jacked up, like on drugs or something. She threw me down on the bed and went down on me again, and when that didn't work, she pulled out a vibrator and started using it on herself," said Sterling, shuddering distastefully.

"All right, I get the picture, let's skip ahead," said Bellamy, suddenly shivering at a visual he really didn't want in his head.

"Did she ever manage to arouse you enough that the two of you were able to have sex?" asked Bellamy.

"No, I was pleading with her, I knew there was no way...she finally kicked me out of her room in my underwear, she told me I was an impotent bastard and she never wanted to see me again," said Sterling.

"So you left," said Salazar.

"Not really," said Sterling, his voice seemed softer, meek.

"What do you mean, not really?" asked Bellamy, looking at him in shock, finally, it seemed they were making a breakthrough.

"I didn't know what to do. I had arrived there in Patrice's car, so I wasn't sure how I would get home. Sadly, I'd left my cell phone in my car at the community center, because I didn't want to be disturbed, so I wasn't sure how I could call for a cab."

"I started walking around the house a little bit, looking for a phone. I walked into the kitchen and used the phone in there. I was just getting ready to walk outside to wait for the cab and Sabine walked in."

"Sabine walked in and saw you standing there?" asked Salazar, hardly able to believe it.

"Yes, I wasn't sure what to do. I was embarrassed. I mean, I was standing there in nothing but a t-shirt and my underwear, when I finally meet the esteemed Sabine Rousseau. I mean the woman is a flipping movie star for God's sake and I'm standing there in her kitchen wearing nothing but an old t-shirt and boxers. I could have vomited then and there," gasped Sterling, his eyes seemingly vacant as he recalled the embarrassing incident.

"What did Sabine do, when she saw you standing there?" asked Bellamy.

"It was weird, she just stared at me oddly for a few minutes. I was scared because her daughter was so crazy and I imagined she thought that I had screwed her daughter, I was afraid she might be angry.

I had no idea what to expect from her. Surprisingly enough, she smiled at me and started walking toward me, I was nervous, because from her point of view, it looked like I was actually doing her daughter." he sighed, miserably.

"Was she mad?" asked Salazar, almost licking his chops, this story was almost too bizarre to be true, though that was what made it believable. He didn't believe Edwin Sterling was worldly enough to make up such a tale of intrigue.

"No, she was...interested," said Sterling, cringing.

"Interested?" asked Bellamy.

"Yes, she introduced herself and asked me if I needed a drink. Boy did I need a drink, so I said "yes". She got out some glasses and poured us both a gin and tonic. I gulped mine down pretty fast, she asked me why I was so nervous, I was literally shaking. I told her I was sorry that she had discovered me in Patrice's bedroom.

"What did she say to that?" asked Bellamy, still jotting notes on his notepad.

"She asked me if Patrice and I truly had sex, because when she walked in the door, our encounter seemed a little theatrical to her. I started laughing, because that was exactly how I would explain it...theatrical."

"I told her that Patrice had been a bit overbearing and rough for my tastes and that I had disappointed her by being too limp to actually have sex," said Sterling, his face approaching a bright shade of red again.

"That must have been embarrassing. Telling a woman that you've admired for many years that her daughter scared you so badly, she'd made you impotent," said Bellamy.

"I was really embarrassed, I told her that I had called a cab, so I could go home, she told me to cancel the cab and stay and have another drink with her," said Sterling.

"So you cancelled the cab and had another drink with her, right?" asked Salazar.

"Yes, I couldn't help it, I guess I've had a secret crush on Sabine Rousseau my entire life. I was finding myself strangely intrigued by her, I felt like we really clicked. We stayed there in the kitchen and talked for a while, she seemed like a very nice and funny lady. I couldn't help but be a little attracted to her. Maybe she noticed...that I had overcome my impotence, I couldn't really help it. She told me that a gentle touch would make me feel much better. I was shocked, I'm not the kind of guys who's fantasies actually come true, but she came over and went down on me, right there in the kitchen," said Sterling, obviously, still fighting his acute embarrassment.

"Did you have a better response to Sabine's touch?" asked Salazar, suddenly fighting the urge to laugh.

"I couldn't help myself. I know she's older, like in her sixties or something, but damn, she was good. Before I knew it, we were doing it, right there on the kitchen counter," said Sterling.

Bellamy had a thought, and it made him cringe painfully, "Did Patrice see the two of you?" he asked.

"No," snapped Sterling, though his face was not convincing.

"Are you certain?" asked Bellamy, he was now having a strange feeling about all of this. Hell hath no fury like a woman scorned. What about a woman who has been betrayed by a potential lover and her own mother? He could only imagine Patrice's rage!

"I don't think so, if she did, she never made her presence known. I guess I was a little too busy to notice. In fact, I may not have noticed if a marching band came through," said Sterling, now finally smiling at the memory of his lovemaking with Sabine.

"So after that, did you call for a cab?" asked Bellamy.

"No, Sabine offered to take me home. She apparently wasn't done with me. She drove me back to my place in her BMW. I invited her inside and we had sex again at my place. She stayed all night, then she got up at five a.m., showered and left," said Sterling.

"Can anyone else confirm your story? asked Bellamy.

"Well, my landlady Lorraine is very nosy. She was peeking out her curtains when Sabine and I pulled up in the parking lot. When I walked past her window, she gave me two thumbs up," said Sterling.

Bellamy scribbled himself a note, to contact the

landlady, and confirm this odd story.

"What about your car? Did you not go back for it? You left it at the community center all night?" asked Salazar.

"My car was the last thing on my mind. Yeah, I left it there, I had a ticket in the morning for leaving it overnight, but I didn't care. Spending the night with Sabine was definitely worth it," said Sterling, his face literally beaming happiness.

"Thank you Mr. Sterling, I believe we have all we need," said Bellamy, standing to shake his hand.

"Do you think it's my fault she's dead?" asked Sterling, his face consumed with guilt.

"You didn't murder her, did you?" asked Salazar.

"No but, Patrice...I don't know. She just seems so unstable. Maybe if she did see me with her mother..." his voice seemed to trail off.

"I see your point Mr. Sterling, but we have to stick to facts here. As unstable as Ms. Bernard seems, it is entirely possible that she had nothing to do with her mother's death," said Bellamy.

Mr. Sterling shook his head numbly and stood to leave.

"We'll contact you if we need anything else," said Salazar.

Chapter 9

Detective Bellamy was staring blankly at the report in front of him. He was so tired, he could no longer concentrate. His eyes were burning and they were so tired, they refused to even try and focus. He could feel his energy waning by the moment and he was wondering miserably, if he would ever catch a break in this case.

So far, all he had was a severely dysfunctional family that had seemingly gone awry, though that in itself, was not a crime. He had his suspicions about who may have murdered Sabine, but so far, he had no hard evidence to back up his theories.

He had essentially ruled out Paloma and Paul, they both had confirmed alibis. They could both prove that they had been at work at the time of the murder. Paloma was definitely too far away to pull off such a task, and neither Paul or Paloma seemed to have a passionate hatred toward their mother, they had both seemingly written her off and preferred to avoid her.

It was becoming quite evident that Patrice had motive to murder her mother, but she too, seemed to have an air tight alibi. If Patrice had been responsible for her mother's murder, it was because she had hired someone or somehow convinced them to do it for her. Bellamy had his doubts about that.

The keypad of the back door had been dusted for prints

and the log checked for any entries into the house, but there were none on the day Sabine had been murdered. Bellamy had checked out everyone who may have had access to the house, including Sabine's personal trainer, Steve, who had been in Italy for the past week, with his male lover.

Bellamy ran his hand through his hair in frustration. He sighed and struggled to concentrate on the report in front of him. It was the phone log from Sabine's residential phone. The report listed all the calls in the past three months that had been made from the Rousseau household, and all calls coming in.

At the very least, it confirmed Edwin Sterling's story about the cab. He had called the cab company at eleven twenty-four, and he called the company again at eleven twenty-nine, when Sabine had asked him to stay and have another drink.

The nosy landlady had confirmed that Edwin had arrived at his apartment just after one, in a silver BMW, in the company of a very elegant, older woman. When the landlady woke up at just after seven, the BMW was gone, just like Edwin had told him.

Bellamy and Salazar now had the arduous task of identifying the source of all the incoming and outgoing calls. Bellamy stood up reluctantly and stretched his back. He would have to work on it tomorrow, he hadn't realized that it was already seven o'clock. Patty would be furious that he had missed Kirby's first baseball game of the season. She had even called this afternoon to remind him, unfortunately, it had still completely slipped his mind.

He sighed miserably, sometimes it was hard to turn your brain off when you worked on a major case like this. Patty didn't understand, she thought he could just stop abruptly at five and forget about whatever twisted murder case he was working on, then just go back to being a dad again.

Most days it was easy enough, but this case had rattled him. There were too many nagging questions in his head. It was a horrifying crime, Sabine had been a star, admired and possibly stalked by her fans.

The department still hadn't released many details to the public, aside from the fact that Sabine had been murdered. If the public knew the gory details of her death, that her heart had been cut out, there would be panic in the city, even though Bellamy knew this was a crime of passion, not a serial killer in the making.

Whomever had murdered Sabine, was sending out a clear message. The person who had committed this crime was a person who had been hurt irreparably by Sabine Rousseau. They had been a friend, a lover or a family member, but it was someone who felt an intimate bond to her. This person had come to her, seemingly to make their peace, but instead, they had exacted their revenge.

The very fact that there was no forced entry into her

home and there was barely a struggle at all, led Doug to imagine that Sabine thought she was in control of the situation, she did not expect this person to harm her. She was caught off guard, and it had lead to her undoing.

Bellamy had admired Sabine Rousseau his entire life, but he was now realizing that she was not the elegant creature he had revered from afar. In her lifetime, Sabine Rousseau had left a trail of carnage in her wake, most evident in her emotionally damaged children. Bellamy felt as if he had really only scratched the surface of her odd, dysfunctional life.

He glanced around his office one last time, then he turned out the light and stepped out into the hallway, the light in Salazar's office was out, he was long gone. It was Friday night, and Chris most likely had a date. Salazar was a ladies man, or so he thought, he was rarely without a new, gorgeous woman on his arm.

Bellamy drove home, alone in his thoughts, the radio was playing classic rock softly, so not to intrude on his thought process. At least he didn't have to encounter much traffic at this hour, he thought to himself.

His mind was wandering as he pondered this disturbing case. He couldn't help but wonder if maybe Patrice had seen her mother with Edwin Sterling. It would be like a sobering slap in the face, if she had. It was Patrice who had brought Edwin back to the mansion, she had spent the entire evening, trying to seduce him, yet he ended up spending the night with her mother, who seemingly had no problems arousing his attention.

If Patrice had seen the two of them together, he had no doubt that she would go off the deep end. Would she flip out enough that she would murder her own mother?

Bellamy sighed miserably, as screwed up as Patrice was that night, it may have been the straw that broke the camel's back. Patrice had been determined to have sex with Sterling. When he couldn't perform, she kicked him out. Patrice had told him after she kicked Sterling out, she had went to bed. Now that he thought about it, Bellamy was realizing that probably wasn't the case. Patrice had grown up in the mansion, high society people just didn't let guests see themselves out, especially virtual strangers. Maybe she had second thoughts about her rudeness, or maybe she wondered if he would pilfer valuables from the house, so she came looking for him, just to make sure he had really left.

Bellamy could only imagine the anger coursing through Patrice's veins when she saw them together, right there in the kitchen. Maybe Sabine had planned it that way, since she was the one who initiated the sexual encounter. Bellamy frowned, he was surprised that there had been no confrontation. Why would Patrice, who seemed to be addicted to drama, let that opportunity slip by, then murder her mother later? Bellamy had no doubt that Patrice would enjoy calling her mother out, catching her in the act like that. Or had Sterling lied and witnessed the whole thing?

Bellamy shuddered miserably. Who knew with this crazy family? When Sabine returned to the house in the morning, maybe her and Patrice had argued. Maybe Patrice had killed her mother in anger, took out her heart and then planted the frozen semen in her vagina to make it look like some sort of a sexual assault.

Bellamy snapped back to reality and was surprised to see he had arrived in his subdivision already, he looked at the clock on the dash, it was almost seven thirty, Patty was going to be pissed!

He walked in the door that connected the kitchen and the garage. Patty and the kids were eating dinner. Patty rolled her eyes and shook her head miserably when he told them all "Hi".

"Dinner's on the stove, help yourself," she snapped angrily.

"Sorry I'm late, this Rousseau murder is taking up a lot of my time," he said, apologetically.

"Hmmm, no kidding," snapped Patty, her voice was dripping with sarcasm.

"Sorry I missed your baseball game buddy," he said to Kirby, who was watching him carefully from his seat. Kirby was eleven and he was a great kid.

"It's OK dad. I figured you were busy," he said.

"I'll be at the next game, I promise," said Bellamy, smiling and ruffling his hair.

"I've got to go," said Samantha, standing to leave.

"Where are you going Sammy?" asked Bellamy, hoping she wasn't leaving just because he was there. Sammy was sixteen, the two of them had been clashing constantly over the past two years. She thought he was too strict, he just worried about her, it seemed like a vicious circle.

"I'm going to Melinda's house, we have to study for American History," she snapped, seemingly almost as angry as her mother.

"OK, I just like to know where you're at," said Bellamy, trying not to sound defensive.

"I can't wait till I'm eighteen and I can move out," cried Sammy, as she left the kitchen in a huff.

"PMS sucks," laughed Kirby, giving his dad a smile.

Bellamy filled his plate and sat down, as soon as he sat down, Patty stood up and started clearing the dinner dishes.

"Kirby, you have homework, go upstairs," snapped Patty.

He gave her a shocked look, but he obediently picked up his plate and put it in the dishwasher, then he went to his room.

"I'm getting really tired of this Doug," barked Patty, still moving around the kitchen in an agitated state.

"I told you I'm sorry. It's just hard to stop when the investigation takes direction. If it were your family member, wouldn't you want me find out who did this to them?" asked Doug.

"You can't play on my sympathies anymore Doug. I have been waiting for eighteen years for you to spend some time with us, I've finally realized, that's never going to happen," snapped Patty.

"Of course it's going to happen. I missed one baseball game, the world's not going to end," he said, trying hard to soothe her.

"Do you realize how many birthdays, how many games, how many milestones, you have missed while our kids were growing up? I've raised these kids by myself, so you can do what you do best, which is solve crimes. I respect your dedication Doug, really I do. But I want someone in my life that wants to spend time with me, spend time with our kids," said Patty.

Doug took a deep, shaky breath, Patty was more upset than he had ever seen her.

"What are you saying?" he asked, almost afraid to hear her answer.

"I want a divorce," said Patty, her eyes cast down at the floor.

"No, that's crazy! We'll work things out. I'll take some time off, we'll take a vacation," said Doug, suddenly panicking.

"No Doug it's over, it's too late to work things out," said Patty, her tone was cold and callous.

"Wait a minute, is there someone else?" asked Doug, at this point he was almost sure there was.

Patty turned around and stared out the kitchen window, her entire body was tensed.

"There is, isn't there?" asked Bellamy, his voice breaking.

"It's Tim," said Patty, her voice fading in embarrassment.

"Tim Wilkey?" cried Doug, barely able to believe it.

Patty nodded her head in shame. Doug felt as if he could barely breathe. Tim was supposed to be his best friend, best friends didn't sleep with their friend's wives!

Tim was Doug's best friend, they had met in college and ended up rooming together. Tim was the county's prosecuting attorney. Doug was so upset, he almost felt sick to his stomach.

"We're moving into his house tomorrow," said Patty.

"You're taking the kids and moving into his house?" cried Doug.

Patty nodded her head, it was as if she were incapable of speech. She couldn't make eye contact with him.

"Do the kids know?" asked Doug, trying to control the emotion in his voice.

Patty nodded her head and began to nervously clean the kitchen again. Doug couldn't believe it was true, he just wanted to scream.

"But..." he didn't know what he wanted to say, on top of everything else, this was like a nightmare he didn't want to face.

"I'm sorry Doug. I'll sleep in the guest bedroom tonight. You won't have to do anything. Tim is already taking care of everything," said Patty, she gave him a wry smile and walked out of the room.

Doug stared at the doorway long after she had walked out. He couldn't think, he couldn't breathe. Finally, he did something he had never done before. He put his face in his hands and broke down in tears.

Chapter 10

Bellamy lay in his bed staring at the ceiling, unable to fall asleep. It was nerve racking enough to be working on the most bizarre murder case of his career, but now Patty had announced that she was leaving him for his best friend, it seemed as if his life was suddenly in shambles!

He lay there wondering how long this had all been going on, yet he had been completely clueless. How could he possibly solve a high profile murder case, when he obviously didn't know what was going on in his own home?

Patty had announced that she was moving out tomorrow. It was too late to change gears, too late to save the marriage that had endured more than eighteen years of ups and downs. Bellamy sighed, of course he hadn't been the perfect husband, but he hadn't been an awful husband either.

The phone on the nightstand rang and jolted Bellamy from his thoughts abruptly. He squinted at the clock, it was nearly one thirty in the morning.

"Bellamy," he snapped, hoping whoever was calling had good news for him, he wasn't sure he could take any more bad news.

"Hey Doug, it's me, Brad," said the voice on the other end of the line. Bellamy grimaced and wondered why the medical examiner was calling him so late.

"Hi, what you got?"

"Well I left early today, so I could go to Bailey's first baseball game and I came back in tonight to finish some tests on the Sabine Rousseau case. The official cause of death was exsanguination, secondary to multiple stab wounds. I have made her official time of death between eleven a.m. and one p.m.," said Brad.

Bellamy frowned, that pretty much ruled Patrice out, if she had truly been teaching her classes that day.

"Thanks Brad," said Bellamy, bidding him goodnight and hanging up the phone.

Bellamy sighed, hopefully with the help of Chris they could figure out some sort of pattern in Sabine's phone records. Doug dragged himself out of bed, he couldn't really sleep anyway, he might as well go over some of the phone records.

He pulled reports out of his briefcase and began the arduous task of trying to find patterns. He looked over incoming and outgoing calls carefully, it seemed most of the calls were between Sabine and her daughter Patrice, it looked as if Sabine had called her an average of sixteen times a day, quite a lot, when you considered that Patrice also had to hold down her full time job.

Nothing else really stood out to Bellamy, until a phone number suddenly appeared just two weeks ago, it was an international number, originating in France. The calls had begun just two weeks ago and continued sporadically, to both Sabine's home and her cell. The last call came in at ten a.m. on the day that Sabine had died. The caller hadn't tried to contact her since that call.

Bellamy highlighted the calls and made some notes to himself. He would get Penny on it in the morning, she would be able to find out who the owner of the phone was, and possibly even their location.

Bellamy was finally able to succumb to sleep, though it seemed the morning rolled around much quicker than he had anticipated. He showered and left the house earlier than usual. He really didn't want to be around when Tim showed up to move Patty and the kids out of the house. It seemed a bit cowardly to him, but he wasn't really ready to face the reality that his marriage was over.

He had stopped off for coffee and was heading toward his office when he heard Salazar calling to him from his office across the hall.

"Hey Doug, you got to see this," said Salazar, waving him into his office.

"What you got?" he asked, Chris' face was flushed with excitement.

"We may have a new player in our little game," said Salazar, grinning broadly.

"I'm not sure I can handle another player at this point," said Bellamy, sighing miserably.

"Check out this new program Penny ran. This tells us everything we need to know about Sabine's phone habits, and you don't have to spend hours going through the print outs manually," said Salazar, beaming with excitement.

"Hmmm, if I had only known this twelve hours ago, maybe I would feel more rested," said Doug, his voice dripping with sarcasm.

"Watch this, there is this international cell phone, the calls started about two weeks ago, the last call was made the day of Sabine's death," said Salazar.

"I know, the phone is from France," said Bellamy, folding his arms over his chest in boredom, he already knew this, he had checked the records manually.

"I ran it down, the phone belongs to an employee of the Paris Ballet, her name is Marielle Benoit, she is from a small town just outside of Toulouse France," said Salazar.

"So Rousseau was possibly a mentor or something. It's not uncommon for a dancer to ask another dancer for advice, maybe she was working on a new project or something," said Bellamy, not convinced that this cell phone would lead them anywhere.

"Well, the best part about this cell phone program is the GPS," said Salazar, flashing him a sly smile.

"GPS?"

"Yeah, you know most cell phones now have a GPS device in them, for apps and stuff like that, right?" said Salazar.

"So what you're saying is, you can tell everywhere Ms. Benoit has been?" asked Bellamy, completely amazed.

"Pretty darn close. The interesting thing was, most of

the phone calls made were from Toulouse, Paris, or somewhere nearby, the two most recent calls, however, where made in Chicago," said Salazar.

"Holy crap! Can we find this chick and bring her in?" cried Bellamy, completely shocked.

"We're working on it, okay? She hasn't made any calls on that phone since, and apparently the phone is no longer on, so we've not been able to access the GPS. We've been monitoring her credit cards, so far, she hasn't made any purchases here in the US, except her rental car at the airport. We know what flight she came in on and according to immigration, she is still here in the states. I got the whole damn force out looking for this chick," said Salazar.

"Do you have a picture?" asked Bellamy, determined to join in the search for this mystery woman.

"Yeah, here's her passport photo," said Salazar, pulling the photo up on computer screen.

Bellamy stared at the image in shock. He couldn't believe what he was seeing.

"Well, I never saw that one coming," said Bellamy, taking a step closer and studying the photo on the screen. "I now believe there is a very valid reason Ms. Benoit traveled all the way to the US to see Sabine," said Bellamy, unable to drag his eyes away from the image on the screen.

"Why?" asked Salazar, staring at him in confusion.

"I am guessing that Sabine is her mother," said Bellamy.

Chapter 11

Bellamy couldn't stop staring at her photo. The photo of Marielle Benoit bore a striking resemblance to Sabine, even more striking than either of her other daughters.

Salazar took a closer look at the photo as well, he was remembering the old black and white photo he had seen at Sabine Rousseau's house. He almost shivered, the resemblance was eerie.

"You keep doing what you've been doing, I'm going to do some research and find out as much as I can about Ms. Benoit," said Bellamy, heading for the door so he could get to work.

"Hey Doug, you OK?" asked Salazar, as he reached the door.

Bellamy paused and cringed inwardly. He'd hoped he would be able to immerse himself in his work before he'd had the chance to think about Patty and where the two of them had gone wrong.

"No, not really...Patty wants a divorce, she's leaving me," said Bellamy, his voice was weak and resigned.

"Don't worry, you guys will work things out," said Salazar, flashing him a forced smile. It was as if he already knew, there was no chance of reconciliation.

"I don't think so, she's taking the kids and moving out. She's moving in with Tim," said Bellamy, sighing miserably.

"Tim? Tim Wilkey!" cried Salazar.

Bellamy couldn't speak, he nodded his head. The pain was too much, he was afraid he would break down in tears again.

"That sneaky bastard. I just saw him a week ago, after court. I asked him how he was doing since Melissa died, he said he was struggling to go on. What a liar!" cried Salazar.

Bellamy sighed, maybe it was his own fault. He hadn't kept in touch with Tim as a friend should. His wife had been diagnosed with advanced breast cancer at the age of thirty nine, she had barely lasted six months after the diagnosis, even though Tim had done everything humanly possible to save her. Her death had hit him hard, Bellamy couldn't believe that now, less than a year later, Patty was moving in with him.

"I'm sorry buddy," said Salazar, giving him a manly hug.

"I know," said Bellamy, turning and walking numbly from the office.

He hadn't seen it coming, but looking back, it all seemed crystal clear. His family had come second to his work. He had put his heart and soul into his career and all Patty and the kids got, was what was left over. Sometimes he had went for weeks, barely seeing them at all when he was working a big case. Patty was right...she had raised the kids all by herself. Bellamy felt like a loser...he couldn't really blame her for leaving, even though he didn't want her to leave.

All he could do was throw himself into his work. Most

of the force was busy tracking leads on the whereabouts of Marielle Benoit. He began doing his research, he wanted to find out everything he possibly could, on Ms. Benoit.

It turned out that Ms. Benoit was a little bit of a loner. She was twice divorced, her most recent marriage ending about six years ago. She was forty six years old and a retired dancer with the Paris Ballet, she currently worked with them as a choreographer. Since her divorce she lived alone, in a small apartment in Paris. She still owned a comfortable home in Toulouse, but the caretaker told Bellamy she hadn't been there in over two years. It seemed as if she didn't have any close friends and she never had any children.

The most disturbing piece of information Bellamy had turned up, was that she had been adopted when she was only hours old. The records showed that it had been a private adoption, not much public information was available. Records showed that Marielle had been adopted by the Benoit family, Jean Paul, who was an accountant, and his wife Claudine, who ran the family's bed and breakfast in Mont Legun, France.

Bellamy tried several times to contact the Benoit family so that he might speak with them, but there was no answer. He had tried Jean Paul at his office in Toulouse and at the Bed and Breakfast, but there was no answer which he thought was odd. Who owns a business, but doesn't have someone there to answer the phone?

He had tried Ms. Benoit's cell phone multiple times, but the calls would go directly to her voice mail. He declined to leave a message. He decided he would call the director of the Paris ballet and get the director's take on what was going on with Ms. Benoit.

The director's name was Marguerite Casson and Bellamy was relieved to find out she spoke very good English. He introduced himself and told her he was calling about Ms. Benoit.

"I am sorry Mr. Bellamy, but Marielle is not here, she has taken leave," said Ms. Casson.

"Do you know where she was going? Was she taking a holiday?" asked Bellamy.

"I am afraid she is off on a wild goose chase," said Ms. Casson.

"Why do you say that?" asked Bellamy.

"Several weeks ago we had a visitor here. Gianni Valducci, the world renowned Italian composer. He came here to see my dancers working on a ballet he composed. He took one look at Marielle and he could not believe his eyes. He told her she was the spitting image of a younger Sabine Rousseau. He went so far as to ask her, in jest of course, if she was Sabine's secret love child," said Ms. Casson.

"What were Marielle's reactions to all of this?" asked Bellamy.

"She told him that she had been born and raised in

Mont Legun and she had her father's nose to prove it," said Ms. Casson.

"Did she not know she was adopted?" asked Bellamy, wondering why someone would keep something so important from her for more than forty six years.

"She had no idea. She called her parents that evening and relayed the story to them, of course, they were both completely horrified. Apparently, they had not planned to tell her the truth, ever. They told her, they were afraid that if she found out she was adopted, she would no longer love them," said Ms. Casson.

"I imagine Ms. Benoit was very upset," said Bellamy.

"She was quite disturbed. She felt betrayed by her adopted family, she felt they had deceived her for many years. In the weeks that followed, Marielle became obsessed about her adoption. It was as if her life suddenly had a mission. She became determined to find out who her real parents were," said Ms. Casson.

"Was she able to find out that information?" asked Bellamy.

"Well apparently the adoption was done quite secretively, this was all done years ago, before people felt the need to have freedom of information. She found a copy of her original birth certificate, but even that was not a wealth of information. It simply listed her parents as SR and JB, an unmarried couple. Of course, she felt that JB was her own father, and SR was Sabine Rousseau," said Ms.

Casson.

"I find that to be highly unlikely, I mean Benoit was a small town guy. How could a small town accountant like Benoit meet up with someone sophisticated and worldly like Sabine Rousseau? I would guess that the two of them were from two different worlds. I think Marielle was drawing some crazy conclusions," said Bellamy.

"Most people might assume that but I beg to differ with you, Mr. Bellamy. Mr. Benoit, now being the older gentleman that he is, may give most people the impression that he is, and always has been, merely a mild mannered, small town accountant. Although those who knew him in his younger days would tell you that Jean Paul Benoit was far from the mild mannered accountant he is today."

"He had been the principal accountant for the Paris ballet back in the day. I did not know him at that time, but I have heard that he spent a great deal of time in Paris, frequenting the clubs, dancing all night. He was quite attractive, so I have heard that he left quite a string of broken hearts behind in Paris. His name had been linked to several of the ballet's dancers, including Sabine Rousseau, if I remember right."

"Of course, most of that was before he married his wife Claudine and settled down in Mont Legun. Claudine was a dear friend of the Benoit family. I believe the marriage was pleasing to both families, but not so much to Jean Paul," said Ms. Casson.

"So for Mr. Benoit, it was basically an arranged marriage then?" asked Bellamy.

"I assume so, from what I've seen, their marriage was basically affection less. I never understood it, I'd always found Mr. Benoit quite attractive, but if the rumors are to believed I guess it was not his fault," said Ms. Casson.

"Meaning what?"

"After years of going three times a week to her quilting club and never producing a single quilt, Jean Paul found out that there actually was no quilting club."

"So what, she was having an affair?" asked Bellamy, that made sense, she'd basically been coerced to marry this man.

"Well, not in the sense you might imagine. She'd been having an affair not with another man, but with a woman. Mr. Benoit finally figured out why his wife seemed to want nothing to do with him, she was a lesbian," said Mrs. Casson.

"When did he find this out?" cried Bellamy.

"Not till after they had been married about five years," said Ms. Casson.

"So they stayed married anyway, even though Mr. Benoit loved women and so did his wife," said Bellamy.

"Their families would have been horrified if they knew, they vowed to stay together and each look the other way when one or the other had needs to be fulfilled. They were both very discrete, most people had no clue," said Ms.

Casson.

"What about Marielle? Did she know," asked Bellamy.

"She never spoke of her parents much, she told me her father had run her out of the house when she was barely eighteen, that was when she came to audition for the ballet. He seemed to love her dearly, I cannot believe that the two of them had some sort of falling out," said Ms. Casson.

"What do you know of the time Sabine Rousseau spent in Paris?" asked Bellamy, trying hard to make sense of all this.

"The Ballet felt quite honored to have Ms. Rousseau spend some time in our troupe. She was also very outgoing and enjoyed the club scene. She was out with a different man every night and she was said to have a very voracious sexual appetite," said Ms. Casson.

"So do you believe it to be possible, that Mr. Benoit and Sabine Rousseau had a love affair?" asked Bellamy, still not convinced.

"Well consider this Detective Bellamy...Marielle does have his nose," said Ms. Casson.

Bellamy sighed in resignation. Everything in this case was too bizarre to be true, why wouldn't Marielle Benoit be Sabine's secret love child?

Bellamy only wondered if this new revelation, a secret that had been concealed from her for more than forty six years was enough to cause Marielle Benoit to go off the deep end and murder, and cut out the heart of her own birth mother. It seemed entirely possible, in his career he had seen people murder for much less.

Chapter 12

Bellamy was sitting at his desk massaging his temples slowly. He'd been fighting a really bad headache all morning, and it was starting to upset his stomach. He had tried several remedies, Advil, coffee, but so far nothing had even taken the edge off of it. Bellamy closed his eyes and sighed in desperation, he was so stressed out, he had decided he wouldn't be surprised at all if he had an ulcer as well.

He jumped in surprise when Penny suddenly burst through his office door nosily, beaming with excitement.

"You'll never believe what I got," she cried excitedly. She was grinning from ear to ear and her face was flushed with excitement. She was obviously hiding something behind her back.

"If it's a gun, I'm using it on myself," said Bellamy, sighing miserably. He couldn't really get excited about anything, his entire life was in the shitter. This case, his personal life, it all sucked as far as he was concerned.

"You're going to kiss me! This is going to be the break you need in your case," cried Penny, she was so excited, she could barely stand still. She held out a plain brown paper bag to him, smiling excitedly.

Bellamy took the bag from her and slowly peeked inside, half expecting a lame practical joke of some sort.

He peered into the bag in confusion, his overwhelmed mind couldn't seem to focus. Why was Penny so excited about a dirty looking turkey baster, and what appeared to be, a used condom. He gave her a look of distaste.

"What the hell?"

"Shit Bellamy, it's what we've been looking for, it's your big break in the case!" cried Penny, her excitement quickly turning to exasperation as Bellamy seemingly couldn't catch on.

"Huh?"

"You poor overwhelmed bastard. For Pete's sake, it's the previously frozen condom and the turkey baster used to put the semen into Mrs. Rousseau," said Penny.

"Holy crap!" cried Bellamy. "This is really it? You've confirmed this?"

"Yep, the semen is a match to the semen found in Sabine, though we still haven't been able to identify who it belongs to. This turkey baster had Sabine's epithelials on it," she told him excitedly.

"Wow, but how...? Where did they find this stuff?" asked Bellamy. The house had been totally clean. The CSI's had checked every trash can in a mile radius, he wasn't sure where else they could have possibly found it.

"Salazar had the CSI's check the dumpsters at the college campus where Patrice works. He's just had a bad feeling about that chick ever since he first met her. They found this stuff in a bag in a dumpster, right outside the

Arts and Sciences building," said Penny.

"Shit, I can't believe I didn't even think of that," sighed Bellamy, shaking his head miserably. He almost winced, it was so simple, Patrice was their top suspect, why wouldn't she take the evidence back to the college and ditch it there? Bellamy wanted to beat his head on his desk in frustration, he should have thought of that. Was he loosing his instincts?

"Wait, you haven't even heard the best part yet," said Penny, beaming excitedly.

"Spill it," said Bellamy.

"There were fingerprints on the turkey baster and they belong to Patrice!" she cried.

"What, are you serious? Really?"

"You can't really be surprised. Of course she did it, the chick is a flippin nut case!" cried Penny. "Now you have the evidence to prove it."

"But it's not possible, she couldn't have. The time of death..."

"The time of death is really only an educated guess. Besides, maybe she slipped away and no one noticed. Witnesses have been known to confirm that people were in places that they truly weren't, just because their minds were telling them they were there, because they are always there. Besides, how do you know someone wasn't covering for her?"

"No, I really don't think..."

"She can't deny it anymore Doug. This evidence is overwhelming, and it's pointing right at Patrice. You have her fingerprints on the turkey baster that was used to put the semen inside her mother! How can she possibly explain that away?" cried Penny.

Bellamy sighed, he wanted to be excited but there was a nagging voice in the back of his mind telling him that Patrice was innocent. She had an alibi, time of death was confirmed to be between eleven and one. He had already confirmed that Patrice had been teaching her classes during that time. It had been confirmed with both staff and students. There was no way she could have made it all the way back to the mansion in noon time traffic to kill her mother. Doug was torn, this evidence was huge, but something in his heart was telling him that Patrice didn't do it.

"Penny I know this evidence seems overwhelming right now and I don't know what is going on, but I am almost certain that Patrice did not kill her mother. There has to be some other explanation," said Bellamy, shaking his head in disbelief.

"I have no doubt she will come up with some crazy story to make herself seem innocent. You fell for her lies didn't you? Bellamy, are you completely losing your mind? I just handed you a freakin trifecta, DNA match semen, epithelials and Patrice's fucking fingerprints on the turkey baster. You better bring her in, you know she did this. If you don't bring Patrice in I'll go over your head, I will take this to the chief," snapped Penny, suddenly angry.

"I didn't fall for her lies, it's just not possible," said Bellamy, still trying to absorb all this new information. He wanted to believe that Patrice had done this and that the case had been solved, but that voice in the back of his brain refused to remain quiet. It was telling him that there were just too many small details that didn't make sense, it had to be someone else.

"You're not going to bring her in, are you?" cried Penny, she had folded her arms across her chest and was staring him down determinedly.

"Of course I'm going to bring her in, but not yet. It's just that..."

"You're crumbling Bellamy, you can't handle the pressure anymore. You're so stressed out, you aren't seeing any of this clearly. I'm sorry Doug, I didn't want to do this, but I'm going to the chief," cried Penny, storming out of his office and slamming the door behind her.

Bellamy sighed miserably as he stared at the door, his life was only going to get more difficult before it got easier, apparently.

Chapter 13

Bellamy's heart was pounding with anxiety as he walked quickly down the hallway. Everyone he passed seemed to look away in embarrassment, no one was willing to make eye contact with him. He shook his head miserably, this was just what he needed on top of everything else that had been going wrong. He was getting the sinking feeling that he was about to be taken off this case.

He'd just been summoned to the chief's office urgently. Of course, he already knew that Penny had went to the chief and complained about him. She was angry, that was understandable. She was convinced that the evidence that she had brought him, left no doubt that Patrice had murdered her mother. Penny was convinced that he should haul Patrice into headquarters like a criminal and question her yet again.

Bellamy shook his head miserably, he just wasn't ready to commit to that. Deep down he knew there was more. He knew that finding Patrice's fingerprints on the turkey baster would be sufficient evidence to convict her, though he still wasn't certain that she had actually done it. He wasn't ignoring the evidence, he just felt there wasn't enough yet.

It was true, Patrice was very book smart, but it was obvious that she was also very naive in a lot of ways. Doug knew that it would be very easy for someone to frame

Patrice and she would be completely clueless. At the moment, she had an airtight alibi for the time of death. She had been teaching her classes. Any number of people could testify on her behalf. Besides, Bellamy was sure that something was up with their mystery woman, Marielle Benoit, but he couldn't prove it yet.

Bellamy stood there staring numbly at the chief's door. The dread he felt in the very pit of his stomach was enough to take his breath away. He didn't want to be taken off the case, he just needed more time. He shook his head resolutely, as if that could shake away the dread he was feeling. He took a deep breath and knocked tentatively.

"Come in," the chief barked. There was no mistaking the irritation in his voice. He was in an especially foul mood.

"Hello," said Bellamy, staring him down confidently. The chief was a man of high ideals. He wouldn't want to deal with someone who wasn't on top of his game. Bellamy refused to give him any inkling that he wasn't on top of his.

"Bellamy, please, have a seat," said the Chief.

Bellamy sat down slowly in the chair in front of his desk.

"The Rousseau murder case. Tell me what you have," barked the chief.

"The evidence and the witnesses have taken us in quite a few different directions, right now I'm trying to figure out the whereabouts of a French woman named..."

The chief was shaking his head miserably and rolling his

eyes. Bellamy cringed.

"Enough already! Bellamy, what the hell's going on here? Penny told me that she just handed you a turkey baster that was used to put previously frozen semen into Sabine Rousseau. Why the hell aren't you on your way to get Patrice Bernard right now?"

"I know what you're thinking, but please just hear me out. There's this French woman..."

"Come on Doug, this turkey baster, not only had Sabine's epithelials on it, but her daughter Patrice's fingerprints all over it. What the hell are you doing, pursuing some French woman who may, or may not have anything to do with this case!" cried the chief, staring him down angrily.

"Well, Patrice has an airtight alibi, any number of people, both students and staff could confirm that she was teaching her classes at the time of the murder. I know that Penny was upset, because she thinks the evidence is pointing to Patrice, but I think..."

"You know what? I don't give a rat's ass what the hell you think anymore Bellamy. We need to solve this case fast. The public is already freaking out about this murder case and they don't even know the gruesome details yet. Do you know what the public opinion of our department will be, if they think there is some sicko out there on the street?

Sabine Rousseau is dead! We now have hard evidence that can convict her daughter, it's case closed as far as I'm concerned. If for some reason the sick details of her death ever slip out to the media, the public will be happy to know that all this insanity was a family matter and there is nothing for them to fear. It's a win-win situation, the daughter will get the psychiatric care she so badly needs, and the world will be a better place," said the chief.

"But Chief, my instincts are telling me that Patrice didn't do it! I want to check out this mystery woman from France. Her resemblance to Sabine is almost eerie. I am getting the sneaky feeling that this woman is possibly a long lost daughter of Sabine's, she just recently found out that she was adopted and now she is here in Chicago, the timing is way too perfect..."

"Bellamy, you're chasing flipping rainbows here! I never heard so much bull crap in my entire life. Are you trying to tell me you're going to trade real DNA and fingerprint evidence for fucking unicorns and fairies?" cried the chief, his face was red and contorted in anger.

"My gut is telling me..."

"Screw your gut Bellamy! Your head is all fucked up right now. You're the best God damn homicide detective I've got, but everyone has their limits. I know what's going on. I know your wife left you for fucking Tim Wilkey. How can you possibly function at the level I need you at when your marriage of more than eighteen years is suddenly over?" cried the chief, staring him down seriously.

"I'm okay," said Bellamy, though he could hear his own voice break when he said it. For some reason it hurts worse, when someone else spells it out to you like that.

"No you're not! If my wife moved the kids halfway across town to live with my best friend, I would be totally fucked up. Come on Doug, take some time off. Take a vacation, God knows you need it," said the Chief, giving him a wry smile.

"No I'm fine," mumbled Bellamy.

"I'm sorry Doug but it's already done, you're off the case. It's too much for one man. Get your personal life in order, get away for a while and I have no doubt you'll come back to me one hundred percent. I need you to be one hundred percent. Like I said, you're the best," said the Chief.

"Don't take me off this case," cried Bellamy, suddenly panicking.

"Please don't make this harder than it already is. I already told you Doug, you're off the case" said the Chief. His face had softened a bit and he actually gave him a wry smile.

He didn't want to take Doug off the case, but it was obvious, he was not himself right now. He needed a break.

Chapter 14

Salazar was leading Patrice Rousseau down the hallway towards the interrogation room in handcuffs. He had picked her up at the college and brought her to headquarters. She had now gone from being the victim's grieving daughter, to their primary suspect.

She had burst into tears, when he read her rights to her and put the handcuffs on. Her face was red and bowed in shame as he led her out to the police cruiser while all her co workers and students all gawked at her in disbelief.

Salazar looked away nervously as he passed his ex-partner, Bellamy in the hallway. The chief had already told him he was taking Doug off the case, as awkward as it was, there was nothing he could do about it. At this point, he wasn't even sure what his feelings were about the whole mess.

Apparently, Doug had refused to bring Patrice in for further questioning, despite new evidence that had been presented to him. Salazar wasn't surprised, he knew his partner well. He wasn't convinced that she did it yet, and he wasn't going to waste a single second interrogating her again until he had a clear direction. That was just how Doug was.

He didn't really agree with Doug's assessment of the situation, but he didn't dare tell him that. His gut had told him right away that Patrice was hiding something, and he had no doubt that Patrice had murdered her own mother. She had a lot to gain with her mother out of the picture. She had a motive and opportunity and though there were still a lot of unanswered questions as far as he was concerned, it pretty much had to be Patrice.

Still, he didn't agree with the chief's decision to take Bellamy off the case. Unfortunately, right now there was nothing he could do about it. He was the new guy in this unit, he couldn't make any waves. He really didn't want his own job in jeopardy.

Besides, he couldn't really argue that Bellamy had too much going on in his life right now. He would be going through a divorce after more than eighteen years of marriage, of course his judgment would be a bit screwed up. Salazar, tried to stay out of the politics of it all. He felt like Bellamy should take a vacation, just take a little time to relax.

Patrice continued to argue with him and resist his touch on her elbow as he led her down the hallway. He was loosing patience with her, he led her into the interrogation room and shoved her haphazardly, into a chair. He really had no desire to interrogate her again, he was so sick of her lies. What he really wanted was to slap the shit out of her, but everything in that room was videotaped, so of course, he couldn't.

Now that they had the new evidence, he wanted to see what kind of lame story she came up with. They had her fingerprints on the turkey baster, how could she possibly explain that away? She murdered her own mother and he was going to nail her!

"I want to know what the hell is going on! Why are you being so obnoxious, why are you treating me like this? I'm grieving, someone brutally murdered my mother. I'm the victim here, why am I handcuffed?" demanded Patrice, narrowing her eyes at him.

"You are no longer just the victim's daughter, you are now our primary suspect," snapped Salazar.

"I told you before, I didn't murder my mother!" shouted Patrice, angry tears were coming to her eyes.

Salazar was unmoved, Patrice was not a normal suspect. She was a skilled actress, she could change her emotions at the blink of an eye, seemingly, however it suited her.

"We now have new evidence that proves to us that you did. Besides, this wouldn't be the first time you have lied to me," seethed Salazar.

"What evidence?" she cried, giving him a steely glare.

"Do you recognize this?" he asked, pulling the turkey baster out of it's plain brown paper bag and holding it out in front of her. She stared at it wide eyed for a few seconds, then slumped back into her chair in resignation. Salazar almost snickered.

"Yes," said Patrice, shrugging nonchalantly.

"This was used to put semen into your mother's vagina after her death," said Salazar, staring her down boldly. He was not going to beat around the bush with her. He was only going to be straight with her, in the hope that she would respond appropriately.

"Yes, I know. I did it," said Patrice, emotionlessly.

"You did it?" cried Salazar, staring at her in shock. He couldn't believe she had admitted it and he was barely able to contain himself, he was so excited.

"I realize now, how sick that would seem to an outsider, but it was something I had to do," she said, bowing her head in shame.

"You're telling me that you had this turkey baster and actually used it to put previously frozen semen into your own mother's vagina?" he cried, the very thought nearly made him sick.

"I had to...I was scared," said Patrice, her eyes were far away and vacant.

"You had to!" boomed Salazar.

"You would never be able to understand. She was a legend, I was trying to protect her. My mother was a terrible slut, but the world didn't need to know that. I was trying to salvage her dignity," breathed Patrice, sighing in resignation.

"I don't understand how tampering with evidence in a murder case, which is a felony, I might add, would salvage your mother's dignity," snapped Salazar.

"I saw her with Eddie the night before. She screwed him, right there in the kitchen. I knew what people would be saying about her, and I didn't want that for her memory," said Patrice, shaking her head miserably.

"It made you mad, when you saw them together, didn't it?" asked Salazar, assessing her carefully. He had guessed it, she had seen Sabine with Eddie. It was probably the straw that broke the camel's back in her dysfunctional relationship with her mother. Her controlling mother, who pretty much forbids her to date, ends up screwing the guy she's been throwing herself at.

"I was furious when I first saw them together, I tried so hard to make Eddie want me..." said Patrice, her voice was fading away, her eyes were far away...vacant.

"When you saw your mother and Eddie together, what did you do? Did you say anything to them? asked Salazar, watching her facial expressions carefully.

"I wanted to. I wanted to say something so badly. I wanted to call my mother a slut, like she always called Paloma, but I couldn't stop watching them..." said Patrice, her eyes were still vacant and far away.

"Then what happened, after they did it?" asked Salazar.

"I don't know, I went to my room," she snapped abruptly.

"I don't believe you Patrice. You mean to tell me you didn't continue to watch the two of them, to see what happened next?" Salazar was prodding her gently, trying to unlock what her frame of mind was when she was watching them.

"No!" snapped Patrice, angrily. Her face was suddenly a bright shade of pink.

"Come on, you were horny and Eddie couldn't get it up for you, but he had no problem getting it up for your elderly mother. How did that make you feel?"

"I didn't feel anything..."

"I doubt I believe that. Do you know what a voyeur is, Patrice?" asked Salazar, his voice was slightly seductive.

"Of course I know what a voyeur is Detective Salazar, I'm a college professor, not a complete moron," she snapped, rolling her eyes miserably.

"Maybe watching your mother and Eddie did a little something for you. Did you go back to your room and fantasize about Eddie?" asked Salazar, gently prodding her with his words.

"Eddie? I went back to my room and fantasized, but it wasn't about that limp dicked little prick," exclaimed Patrice.

"Maybe the reason you didn't confront your mother is you were turned on. Did you touch yourself, when you went to bed that night?" asked Salazar, hoping to fling open the doors of her emotion. She was hiding something, and he was determined to find out what it was.

"Detective Salazar, if you are asking did I masturbate, the answer is yes, but in my fantasy, I was with that other detective...Bellamy," said Patrice, licking her lips and smiling at him, she would not be intimidated.

Salazar almost shuddered, she was staring him down arrogantly, not threatened one bit by the shiny silver badge he wore on his vest.

"You were jealous of your mother, so you killed her, you waited until Eddie left and then you killed her for stealing your action," said Salazar, cautiously trying to move her attention away from Bellamy. Patrice was so inappropriate, he wondered if she was just messing with him, in an attempt to throw him off.

"That's a bit ridiculous detective, I mean I really wouldn't consider Eddie to be action. I mean sure, I would have liked to at least got laid that night, but Eddie wasn't really my type. He was desperate and so was I, but I seriously doubt he could have got me off, he was such a nervous little guy.

Of course, he was OK for my mother because she was old. But Detective Bellamy, now he's my type. Besides, I could tell by the way he looked at me, he wanted me. There's a lot of guys out there that secretly find fat girls intriguing and sexy," said Patrice, raising her eyebrows at him seductively. Salazar resisted the urge to roll his eyes. He was trying to appear emotionless, even though Patrice was shocking him, with her overly suggestive dialogue.

"You murdered your mother because she was controlling you. Having sex with Eddie was just another one of her pranks to control you. It was like a slap in the face wasn't it? Your sixty six year old mother was fucking the guy you couldn't even arouse. That had to make you feel like shit," cried Salazar, staring her down boldly.

"My mother has always made me feel like shit, it was her way of making herself feel better," cried Patrice, shaking her head miserably.

"She made your entire life so miserable, you killed her, then you staged the scene of the murder to make it look like someone else had been there. It was a perfect plan, since both your siblings are estranged from the family you would inherit everything," said Salazar.

"I told you detective, I didn't kill her. I admit, there are times when I considered it, but I was raised a Bernard. I would never disgrace my father's name in that way. In fact, I did all this simply to protect my father's good name. I am guilty of tampering with evidence, but that is all. I did not kill my mother," said Patrice, staring back at him calmly.

"Really?" cried Salazar.

"I already told you, I didn't kill her, I don't know who did it, I assumed it was Eddie. When I came home from my classes and found my mother's body that afternoon, I was horrified. My mother was lying there in the study...she was bloody. I could tell that she'd had someone over, I mean who else could it be? She'd already insulted and alienated all our friends.

I was scared, but I was moving closer, I wanted to see if there was anyway possible that she was still alive. As I got closer I could see that her blouse was open and her chest was gaping open. I was shaking so bad at this point I could no longer walk. I crawled the rest of the way to her and saw that whomever had killed her, had cut out her heart. Suddenly, I understood. It was a lover who had killed her, exactly like she deserved," said Patrice, her face was smooth and expressionless.

"What do you mean, exactly like she deserved?" asked Salazar. He was biting his lower lip in concentration. He could almost believe this story, he was wondering why Patrice hadn't told them all this from the very beginning.

"I wasn't even sad when I saw her lying there. I knew right away that Eddie had killed her. It was only a matter of time before she offended the wrong person. My mother liked to use men, there were just objects to her. She didn't want a relationship with them, so she would hurt them when she was done with them, just so they wouldn't call her again."

"What do you mean, hurt them?"

"It's so easy detective, men have incredibly fragile egos. The easiest way to ensure that a man never calls you again is to insult his masculinity. A man's entire state of mine is tied to his penis. My mother was a master at ditching men. If Eddie had become infatuated with her, the first thing she would do is insult his masculinity. Maybe she told him he had a tiny little dick, I'm not really sure. She did that kind of crap all the time," said Patrice, giving him a little shrug.

"Okay, let's just say that all this really happened, your

mother insulted Eddie's masculinity and he was so angry he murdered her. But I still don't understand, why did you tamper with the crime scene?" asked Salazar, still not sure if he believed any of this.

"I was afraid you would find Eddie's semen in her. I was scared that Eddie would be linked to both me and my mother. I mean, plenty of people knew we had went out.

I was only trying to protect my mother's reputation. I wanted my mother to be remembered as the elegant woman she had been years ago...being murdered by a one night stand is tacky. A random sexual assault and murder though, is something I could live with. It would make my mother the victim of a random attack, not a disgusting slut who had actually enraged her lover to the point that he had cut her heart out."

"But still..." Salazar was frowning, this whole ordeal was making him feel a bit nauseated.

"I guess I just panicked when I saw her laying there. I went and got the semen out of the freezer and thawed it out. I found the turkey baster and put it in her, so that it wouldn't be Eddie's semen that was found," said Patrice, her voice suddenly quivering with emotion.

"You just happened to have semen in your freezer?" asked Salazar, thinking that this chick was about the weirdest he had ever met.

"Yes," she said, eyeing him seriously.

"Who's semen is it? Do you even know?" asked Salazar,

dangerously close to loosing his cool. This chick was flippin nuts!

"It's my brother's," she told him, unemotionally.

"Jesus Christ! Why were you saving your brother's semen in the freezer?" cried Salazar, almost afraid to hear her answer.

"I found it in the trash can when he and his wife stayed at the house for our Dad's funeral. I figured it might come in handy some day," said Patrice.

"You figured it might come in handy some day?" cried Salazar.

"I guess I'm a bit of a collector," said Patrice, flashing him a sly smile.

"A collector of what?" asked Salazar.

"Well isn't it obvious Detective Salazar? I collect semen. I have 46 specimens in my freezer at work. I thought using my brother's semen would throw the department off the most. It was quite unfortunate his DNA wasn't in the system. That would have been hilarious! Your people would have been totally freaking out!" cried Patrice, giggling like a little girl.

Salazar couldn't help it, he was staring at her numbly. This chick was completely nuts. He suddenly felt as if he could hardly breathe. He couldn't do this anymore, he was backing slowly out the door. A uniformed police officer was standing right outside the door as he turned and stormed out.

"Send the CSI's back out to the University. I want them to search Ms. Rousseau's personal freezer," he barked. He was shuddering in disbelief. He had totally underestimated her, Patrice Bernard was much sicker than he had ever imagined.

Chapter 15

The chief shivered as he watched the videotaped interview with Patrice again. His eyes were fixed on the TV screen, almost unblinking. If he hadn't seen the interview with his own eyes, he never would have believed it.

Patrice's arrogant boast had sounded like a far-fetched story, but she hadn't been lying, the CSI's had found exactly what Patrice had told them they would find. Forty six used condoms, carefully packaged in zip lock sandwich bags and carefully labeled with the donor's name. The chief shook his head numbly, his eyes still glued to the video flashing on the screen in front of him. He had watched it three times and he still couldn't believe it. I mean really, who fishes used condoms out of the trash can and freezes them, "just in case".

He'd seen some screwed up people in his time, but Patrice Bernard had them all topped. Just seeing a dead body in their study would be enough to send most people into hysterics. If that dead body were their own mother, no matter how strained the relationship, most people would find themselves barely able to function.

How could someone actually walk into a room, find their mother's murdered body and actually have the frame of mind to go to their freezer, pick out a semen sample, then use a turkey baster to implant false evidence into their own mother's vagina? In fact, who would even have a frozen semen sample in their freezer in the first place? Sick...

The chief had studied everything, he'd gone back through every interview and every piece of evidence. Edwin Sterling couldn't have murdered Sabine, his alibi was airtight. He had been at work between eleven and one on the day of the murder. There was actual video evidence to confirm it via his finance company's security footage.

Besides, the man was a model citizen, Sterling's boss had nothing but praise for him. He was a diligent worker who hadn't missed a day of work in more than five years and he rarely ever took more than twenty minutes for lunch. The day of Sabine's murder, he hadn't left the office at all. He'd eaten a ham and cheese sandwich in the company's break room, it was all on security video.

The chief sighed miserably, now he was convinced that Patrice hadn't murdered her mother either. Yes, there was definitely something wrong with her. Yes, she was sick and twisted. Yes, she had tampered with and planted false evidence at their crime scene, but both staff and students could vouch that she was on the college campus between eleven and one, there was scarcely enough time in her packed schedule to complete the drive back to the mansion in mid day traffic, let alone, murder and cut out the heart of her mother. At this point, the chief had no choice but to believe it was someone else who had murdered Sabine.

Chief was realizing that he had pulled Bellamy off the

case prematurely, but he hated to admit he was wrong. It wasn't completely his fault, he had been under pressure from the mayor to solve this case quickly. Of course, this was Sabine Rousseau who was a beloved local icon and she had been brutally murdered. He knew the sooner they had the person responsible behind bars, the happier the public would be.

Chief was rubbing his chin uneasily, he was suddenly worried about this French chick that nobody seemed to be able to find. So far they had no evidence that she had anything to do with it...but things were about to change.

"Chief, I have something you'll want to see," said Penny, approaching him excitedly.

"What have you got?" he asked, almost unwilling to drag his eyes from the video screen, Patrice Bernard was still spinning her web of lies on the screen and for some strange reason, it fascinated him.

"I have a hair in the Sabine Rousseau case," said Penny.

"New evidence?" he asked, turning to her, suddenly interested.

"Not really new," said Penny, she was frowning in embarrassment.

"What do you mean, not really new? When was this found?" asked the chief, looking at her completely puzzled. The CSI's had gone over the entire crime scene with a fine toothed comb. Everything they had submitted had been sent to the lab to be tested. New evidence didn't just fall out of the sky this late in the game.

"It was found during the initial investigation. It was brought to me with the rest of the samples. It's all my fault, I didn't test it, because it looked just like all the others I had tested. It was pale blonde, it looked exactly like the ones that belonged to Sabine and Patrice. I just assumed that it belonged to one of them," said Penny, almost whining.

"But it didn't belong to either of them?"

"No, but it has multiple alleles in common to both of them," said Penny.

"A relative?" asked the chief.

"I'm so sorry, I feel really bad Chief. I was wrong and Bellamy was right. This French lady really is Sabine Rousseau's daughter, and now we can place her inside the house," cried Penny.

"Well, I guess I have no choice but to put Bellamy back on the case," said the chief, smiling at Penny.

"I'm really sorry Chief, it's all my fault, I should have tested all the hairs right away, I assumed..."

"Yes, I know. See what happens when we assume? You've gone and made an ass out of you and me," said the Chief, standing and walking out of the room.

Chapter 16

Bellamy sat on his deck and took a long swig of his beer as he gazed around his empty yard. He swirled the much too warm, amber liquid around in it's dark amber bottle in boredom. He had already distractedly peeled off the label. Bits of it lay all around his chair as he stared blankly out across his freshly cut grass.

It seemed weird to be sitting there with no place to go and nothing to do. It had been a long time since he had any leisure time. If he wasn't working there had always been something to do, a chore, a kid that needed to be run to a soccer game, or the library...something.

Bellamy sighed in despair, he never did well with leisure time, he liked being busy. Being busy kept his mind off his completely screwed up life. The grass was cut, the walk was swept and his family was gone. They had moved out of the house and in with his former best friend Tim on Saturday. It seemed like a nightmare his body refused to wake up from.

Now there was no one to play catch with in the back yard, no teenage daughter to roll her eyes and scowl when he gave her a curfew. No wife to stomp around angrily in the kitchen when he came home late. They had even taken the stinking, annoying, dog that he had never cared much for, but was suddenly missing. Bellamy was free, he could do whatever he wanted to. He was completely miserable.

He was completely lost in his thoughts and misery as he stared out across his freshly cut lawn. He was suddenly startled by the sound of music and soon he was vaguely aware that his cell phone was ringing.

"Bellamy," he barked, when he snapped it open.

"Detective Bellamy, this is Madame Casson, I hope this is a good time to talk to you. I hate to bother you, but I have some distressing news to tell you about Marielle Benoit," said the anxious voice on the other end of the phone line.

"I'm very sorry Ms. Casson, I am no longer on the case," said Bellamy, he almost had to force himself to say the words, it was almost too painful to be true.

"I am very sorry, I did not know who else to call. I wanted to make sure that your department was aware of the tragic news," said Ms. Casson.

"What news?" asked Bellamy, his curiosity was officially aroused, even though he was off the case.

"Has the Gendarmerie Nationale contacted your department yet?" asked Ms. Casson.

"Gendarmerie Nationale?" cried Bellamy, in surprise.

"The Gendarmerie Nationale is our law enforcement agency, in the smaller villages," said Ms. Casson.

"Why would the Gendarmerie National be contacting me? I realize she is French, but Ms. Rousseau's murder was on American soil, they..."

"That may be true Detective Bellamy, but things are

much worse than I would have guessed with Marielle. It seems as that her parents had not been heard from in days, no one had seen them, no one was able to reach them by phone. Finally, a concerned friend broke into their cottage in Mont Legun in hopes that maybe they had taken a well deserved vacation and that all her worries about them were for naught. Unfortunately, the poor woman got the shock of her life. She found Mr. and Mrs. Benoit murdered in their own bed, they both had their throats slit, and they had their hearts cut right out of their chests," said Ms. Casson, grimly.

"Holy crap!" cried Bellamy.

"That is right Detective, I believe that Marielle has lost her mind. She was shocked when she heard the news that she had been adopted. She had been lied to for forty six years, she feels as if everyone has deceived her for many years and now she apparently feels she has a score to settle with the people she believes are responsible for her unhappiness," said Ms. Casson.

"Thank you for calling, I'm going to head to the office right now," said Bellamy, heading into the house to change his clothes.

His body was suddenly charged with adrenaline and his mind was going a dozen different directions at once. Should he just go to headquarters and approach the chief with this new information, or should he call first? He knew no one was very happy with him right now, but the fact that

Ms. Benoit had murdered her adoptive parents in the very same manner as Sabine was found murdered would be overwhelming proof that Marielle had done it. No media agency here had been given the information that Sabine Rousseau's heart had been cut out so the general public had no idea. There was no way Ms. Casson could have known details of Sabine Rousseau's murder.

The phone rang once again as he was finishing up, this time the caller ID showed that it was Police headquarters. Bellamy snatched up the phone and answered it, almost holding his breath. He was afraid that he would be shot down, once again.

"Bellamy," he snapped, as confidently as his anxious voice would allow.

"It's me, Chief," said the voice on the other end of the phone.

"Yeah," said Bellamy swallowing nervously.

"I want you back on the Rousseau case. I was wrong...there has been a new development," said Chief.

"So the Gendarmerie Nationale has contacted you?" asked Bellamy, almost breathing a sigh of relief.

"The genda what? No...we have new DNA evidence. The French woman you mentioned, we can place her there in the mansion," said Chief, though he now sounded confused. "What's that Genda something Nationale, you were talking about?"

"The Gendarmerie Nationale is a French law

enforcement agency. I just got a call from the Ms. Casson of the Paris Ballet. She told me that Marielle Benoit's parents were found murdered in their home, their throats were slit, and their hearts were cut out, just like Sabine's," said Bellamy.

"Shit!" cried the chief, he suddenly seemed to be at a loss for words.

"I'm coming in," said Bellamy, quickly before the chief changed his mind.

Bellamy arrived at headquarters in record time, apparently a detective with the Gendarmerie Nationale was en route to Chicago right now to offer his assistance in the case. He was bringing the case file from France so that the two cases could be compared.

The entire department was working tirelessly to find Marielle Benoit. Bellamy now felt an overwhelming sense of fear that they would not be able to find her. If she had no desire to return to France she could fade into the crowd in Chicago, maybe get a new identity, change her appearance.

Salazar had determined that Ms. Benoit had last used her credit card to rent a car at O'Hare airport just three days ago. It was a black Toyota Camry so of course, it wouldn't really stand out at all. The press and police departments nationwide had been notified, but Bellamy was not optimistic. In a rental car, Marielle could disappear anywhere.

He wondered why she was still here. Did she think she

was safer in the states rather than France, or was she not done yet? If she still felt that the score wasn't settled, who else would she possibly target?

Bellamy went straight to his office and got to work calling anyone he thought might be able to help them track down Marielle. Not quite an hour had passed and suddenly Salazar had appeared in his office doorway. He was accompanied by a man in a dark pinstripe suit. Bellamy assumed that this was the French detective they had been expecting.

"Doug, this is Thomas Dumonde. He is a detective with Gendarm, Gend...ahh, he's with the French police. He is here to help us in any way possible," said Salazar, as the man approached him and shook his hand.

"What can you tell me about your case in France?" asked Bellamy, as he gestured to the man to sit in one of the chairs in front of his desk.

"We only found the crime, days after it was committed. She murdered both the Benoits in their bed. Their throats had been slashed and both of their hearts had been cut out. She apparently slipped away unseen and traveled here, where she did the same thing to Ms. Rousseau. In fact, the bodies were discovered on the very same day, though by the time our victims were discovered, they had already been dead for several days.

It was a concerned friend who finally broke into their little cottage to look for them. The poor woman was completely horrified when she found her dear friends murdered in their bed, their hearts brutally cut out. The woman is so distressed, she feels she will have nightmares of her discovery the rest of her life!" said Detective Dumonde.

"What can you tell me about Marielle Benoit?" asked Bellamy.

"Marielle was an accomplished ballerina, one of the top dancers in the Paris ballet for years. As odd as it seems now, she had worshipped and been compared to Sabine Rousseau her entire life, as she resembled her quite a bit and their dancing was also quite similar.

Marielle was a perfectionist, she craved perfection not only in her dance but in her personal life as well. I have been told that her house was compulsively clean and she showered multiple times a day, sometimes to the point where she had scrubbed her skin raw.

It has been rumored that men were enchanted with her beauty, but they were soon repulsed by her odd compulsions," said Thomas, shrugging.

"What compulsions? Her cleanliness?" asked Bellamy.

"Apparently the cleanliness was the least daunting of her numerous compulsions. The others were...well, according to the rumors her other compulsions were bordering on insanity."

"What were they?" cried Bellamy. He was suddenly fascinated. He wondered if OCD was genetically inherited because Sabine had also been fastidious with her grooming and housecleaning. It would be quite compelling if her birth child had the same compulsions, even though Sabine had not raised her.

"She had no children, because of her dancing career. Though she had multiple lovers, she was apparently quite anxious about becoming pregnant. This fear of pregnancy apparently fueled some odd rituals for Ms. Benoit, even though all the men I spoke with believed that she was addicted to sex," said Detective Dumonde.

"What do you mean, addicted to sex?" asked Salazar, completely intrigued, because he too, seemed to be addicted to sex.

"She was a classy lady, so all the men felt the need to wine and dine her. When she had an attraction to a man, she didn't want to be taken out to dinner, she didn't want to make small talk. She wanted to take them back to her place and get it over with, it was very impersonal, she wanted no relationship at all, only sex," said Thomas.

"Hmmm, sounds a bit like her birth mother, Sabine," said Bellamy, stroking his chin thoughtfully. "What else?"

"She had no shortage of men pursuing her, of course she was gorgeous, men were drawn to her, it was her method of preventing pregnancy, that was what usually drove the men away," said Dumonde.

"What method was that? Abstinence...because that would definitely drive me away," said Salazar, laughing hysterically. Dumonde gave him an odd look, he was obviously a no nonsense kind of guy and he did not appreciate Salazar's little joke.

"I told you, this woman was addicted to sex, though it was more about her, than it was the man. She refused to let any man...how shall I say it...release his pleasure inside her."

"Oh..." said Salazar, frowning.

"She frustrated a great many lovers by insisting that they finish their business into a plastic bag, whether they were wearing a condom or not," said Dumonde, assessing them both emotionlessly.

"I have heard of that...women being so obsessed about avoiding pregnancy that they practice the withdrawal method and masturbate their partner to climax," said Bellamy.

"I am sure that her partners would have been a bit more satisfied with that method. She made all her partners bring themselves to their climax, she refused to touch them, once they had been inside her. Like I said before, her obsession with cleanliness was very intense. She was very adamant that the semen go into the plastic bag."

"Oh God, the whole family just has a creepy fascination with semen and plastic bags...it's just unnatural," said Salazar, grimacing.

"I admit, it is very strange. Did she save their semen, freeze it in plastic bags?" asked Bellamy, thinking he was seeing a pattern here.

"Not to my knowledge, my understanding was she had a phobia of semen. She didn't want it to touch her, her clothing, or her bed linens. Thus, the plastic bag," said Dumonde.

"That is so fucked up," said Salazar, shaking his head in amazement.

With that, the office door was flung open and Penny burst in excitedly.

"Sorry to interrupt," said Penny, nodding to Detective Dumonde, anxiously. "We have a hit! Marielle used her credit card in Billings, Montana to get a cash advance!" cried Penny, beaming excitedly.

"Billings Montana, what the hell? Did she suddenly have the urge to become a freaking cowboy?" cried Salazar, looking completely thrown off.

"Oh my God, she's going after Paloma!" cried Bellamy.

"How do you figure?" asked Salazar.

"She can't fly to Seattle and she knows it. She's been flagged, airport security would apprehend her in a minute, but she can take her rental car anywhere pretty much undetected," cried Bellamy.

"Why the hell would she want to go after Paloma?" cried Salazar, still confused. "What the hell did Paloma ever do to her?"

"Paloma didn't do anything to her, but my guess is Marielle still feels wronged. She was abandoned by her birth mother who went on to have another baby just a year later, who she raised in the spotlight and to all outsiders, appeared to adore.

Marielle was so shocked by the news of her adoption, surely, by the time she put two and two together, she felt a distant bond to Paloma. To the outside world Paloma was living the dream, her mother thrust her into the spotlight, got her small parts in movies and musicals. Eventually pushing her into becoming engaged to British noble, Arthur Barrington. To anyone on the outside, it would seem like Paloma was living a charmed life, though Paloma wasn't as happy as everyone had imagined. If Detective Dumonde is correct and Marielle worshipped Sabine, then she had probably also followed her daughter in the spotlight.

Maybe since Marielle resembled Sabine so much she had fantasized that she truly was her daughter, that she was the one in the spotlight all those years, not Paloma. Imagine what a shock it was, when more than forty six years later, she finds out she really was Sabine's daughter, I mean she's already killed everyone else responsible for her pain," said Bellamy.

Salazar, Penny, and Detective Dumonde were all staring at him, with shocked looks on their faces. Unfortunately they knew he was right. Paloma Webster was in grave danger.

Chapter 17

A hush had fallen over the entire room as they considered the wrath of Marielle's misplaced anger. It really didn't matter what Paloma's life had truly been like, Marielle's perceptions were clouding her brain.

Bellamy turned to his computer and pulled up Mapquest. He typed in "Chicago to Seattle" to try and figure out what route Marielle might be taking, in her quest to get to Paloma.

"Billings, Montana," he said, turning the computer monitor around so he could show the others.

They all crowded closer to the monitor and peered at the tiny dot on the map that indicated it was Billings, Montana. Bellamy could feel his heart rate increasing with the adrenaline that was being infused into his body. The number of miles she had covered in so short a time confirmed to Bellamy what he had already feared. Marielle's anger had completely consumed her, she had already killed three people and she apparently wasn't done yet.

Marielle had already traveled an enormous distance to try to reach her half sister, whom she didn't know at all, but already detested. Bellamy almost shivered at the thought of the anger he knew was lurking in Marielle Benoit, an anger that she probably felt was completely justified.

Marielle didn't seem to realize, she had already exacted

her revenge on the people who had hurt her. Paloma and Marielle were both nothing but unfortunate victims of the society their mother had lived in more than forty years before. Today things would be different, an illegitimate child wouldn't be such a big deal. Back then though, Sabine probably thought her career would be ruined forever.

"We need stop her, we need to get to Seattle," cried Bellamy. "Penny, I want every branch of law enforcement searching that stretch of I-90 with a fine toothed comb, she's in a black Toyota Camry, here's the license plate number," he handed her a small, worn scrap of paper.

Penny nodded at him numbly, her amber brown eyes were as wide as saucers. It was hard to get Penny shook up but obviously, the thought of Marielle Benoit going after one more person, killing them and cutting their heart out, had her completely rattled.

"Do we know approximately what time that charge was made?" he asked her.

"About two hours ago," said Penny.

"Two hours! Holy Christ, she could be anywhere by now!" cried Salazar, rolling his eyes miserably.

"Montana is a huge state, Billings is right in the middle, it's going to take her hours just to get out of Montana, unless she suddenly sprouts wings," said Bellamy, staring at them all very seriously. "Like I said, let's get everyone in law enforcement on that stretch of I-90 and find Benoit. We have got to get her, before she gets to Paloma,"

With that, Bellamy stood up, gave the others a terse nod, and strode into the chief's office.

"Hey Doug," said the Chief, standing up as he walked into the room. "I'm sorry I ever doubted you, it's good to have you back."

"I admit, I haven't been one hundred percent myself, but I'm back, and I'm going to get Marielle Benoit if it kills me," said Bellamy.

"What's the story? Is the French agent here?" asked the chief.

"Yeah, his name is Thomas Dumonde, I think he's going to be a great help on our case. Marielle is on the run. We just got a hit on her credit card in Billings, Montana," said Bellamy.

"Billings, Montana? What the hell?" cried Chief.

"I know, that's exactly what Salazar said. I'm almost one hundred percent sure she's after Paloma," said Bellamy.

"Why in the hell would she be after Rousseau's oldest daughter? I can't imagine that the two have even met." said Chief.

"One by one, she's settling the score with those who she feels have wronged her. Maybe Paloma didn't physically do anything to Marielle, but I imagine Marielle is still very jealous of her. Marielle is the daughter who was basically thrown away, the one that was cast into a modest life and forced to fight her way up in the harsh world of dance."

"Paloma, on the other hand, was Sabine's legitimate

daughter, and the reluctant dancer in the spotlight. Sabine thrust Paloma into the ballet and the theater, then finally into an engagement with a British nobleman she did not love. As far as Marielle could tell, Paloma was the lucky one, surrounded by fame and fortune. Marielle probably watched Sabine her entire life, never knowing that she was her eldest daughter. She struggled through life, while Paloma was given everything on a silver platter, or so it seemed. Imagine Marielle's surprise when she realized that Sabine was her real mother," said Bellamy.

"OK, I see that Paloma is in danger, what do you want from me?" asked the Chief.

"I think that Salazar and I should be there in Seattle, to apprehend her when she arrives," said Bellamy.

"That's ridiculous, let the locals nab her. What do I need to fly your asses up there for?" cried the chief.

"She's going to kill again and this time, I guarantee, it will be her half sister," said Bellamy, his voice raising in anger.

"It is not your job to fly halfway across the country and save her. Call Paloma and warn her. Let the locals pick up Marielle, there's no money in the budget for me to send you two clowns to freaking Seattle," said the Chief, laughing.

Bellamy stared him down seriously, he wasn't laughing. He felt the need to finish this case personally. He wanted to apprehend her and prevent her from getting to her next intended victim. "Fine, I'll pay my own way, but I'm going to

Seattle," said Bellamy, turning and heading for the door.

"That's fine with me, pay your own way to freakin Seattle. In fact, I hope you spend all your fucking money before Patty gets one freakin cent. You might as well fly fucking first class you arrogant bastard!" cried the chief, as Bellamy walked out and slammed the door behind him.

Chief shook his head miserably. He hated to be angry with Bellamy but he was just so infuriating sometimes. Unfortunately, that was Bellamy. He was good, but at times he thought he was a god. He didn't think anyone else could do the job as well as he could. He had no doubt that Bellamy would fly to Seattle and apprehend Marielle Benoit himself. He smiled to himself and shook his head, that's what made him such a damn good cop.

Bellamy stormed back into his office, he was angry but exhilarated. In the back of his mind he had known that the chief could never authorize the department to pay for his expenses to go to Seattle, but he wanted so badly to bring this case to an end and he didn't trust God knows who in Seattle to do it.

It didn't matter, he was going to do it, his own heart was telling him he had to do it. He couldn't let Marielle Benoit take one more life, she had already hurt so many people. He had already decided, he was going to Seattle to end all this. He picked up the phone and dialed Paloma's office.

"Puget Sound Pediatric group, how may I help you?" said

the voice on the other end of the line.

"Hello, this is Detective Bellamy with the Chicago Police. I need to talk to Dr. Webster, it's quite urgent," said Bellamy.

"I'm sorry sir, Dr. Webster is out of town. Do you have a medical emergency?" asked the voice.

"No, I just need to talk to Dr. Webster. I'll try her cell phone," he said, hanging up the phone.

He dialed her cell phone, it went straight to her voice mail. He left a short message, then he tried her home number. Once again there was no answer, though he chose not to leave a message on her answering machine at home.

He sat down at his computer and got on line and made arrangements for the first possible flight to Seattle. He also booked a room in a hotel that wouldn't be too far from Paloma's Bainbridge Island home. Soon there was a tentative knock at the door.

"Come in," cried Bellamy.

Salazar stuck his head in the door, and gave him a quizzical look. Bellamy knew right away why he was there, he looked hurt.

"Hi bud, what's up?" he asked, even though he was pretty sure Salazar had gotten the news that he was going to Seattle without him. He hated to hurt his partner's feelings but this was something he had to do, he would not ask his partner to spend his own money to go with him.

"Chief says you're going to Seattle without me," said

Salazar.

"Well, I'm going invited or not. The department won't pick up the tab, so I'm paying my own way. You're welcome to do the same, I'm just thinking the women of Chicago wouldn't be able to survive without you for a couple of days anyway," said Bellamy, giving him a sly smile.

"You don't need to go, you know," said Salazar.

"Yes I do Chris. Right now this case is my life. I want to be there for the grand finale. I mean look at me, I'm lost. My family is gone, what else do I have?" asked Bellamy.

"But you don't have to go, you're going to get the credit anyway. I mean you've already solved the case, all they have to do is apprehend her and the case is over. You should be congratulated, you probably saved Paloma's life. It was you who looked past the obvious, you weren't willing to give up, yet everyone else, including me, thought the case was solved. We had all decided that Patrice had done it," said Salazar.

"It's not over yet," said Bellamy.

"Listen Doug, this chick is dangerous. At this point, she has nothing to lose and that makes her all that much scarier. Besides, you're not as young as you used to be..."

"Spare me the speech. I know exactly how old I am. I don't think you realize that I have to do this. Please, don't you worry about me," said Bellamy.

"I am worried about you. You don't know your limitations any more," said Salazar, his face was serious.

"I know my limitations. I just refuse to acknowledge them...there's a difference," said Bellamy, flashing him a sly smile.

"You're a crazy ass bastard, you know that?" asked Salazar.

"Yeah, I know..."

Chapter 18

Bellamy's flight arrived in Seattle on time and without incident. He managed to get a cab at the airport and he was now heading toward his hotel in a cold drizzle. He glanced around at all the cars slowly wending their way down the rain soaked streets of the city. They crawled along with their headlights on in the middle of the day. He wondered how anyone could live here, with just over forty sunny days a year, how could anyone possibly stand it? Though people had a variety of reasons why they moved anywhere, or even stayed where they had been born. Sometimes he wondered how he had ever ended up in Chicago.

He had been born and raised in Tampa Florida and he'd graduated from the University of Tampa. Tampa was a city he had loved from the day he was born. He had hundreds of happy memories of his childhood. Weekends at the beach, summer days on his father's sailboat, it was a far cry from the windy city he had ended up in.

He had moved to Chicago to be with his true love, Patty. He had just graduated from Tampa U and he had applied to large police departments all over the US. He wanted to get a few years experience in a big city, then he planned to return to Florida. Getting on with the Chicago police force had been like a dream come true, there was plenty of action twenty four hours a day.

He ended up meeting Patty one evening and his plans of returning to Florida someday were all forgotten. He couldn't believe a woman as smart and beautiful as Patty would even give him the time of day, but she agreed to go out with him and it was the beginning of a whirlwind romance. Before he knew it, he was married, with a house in suburbs, two kids and an annoying Basset hound. Everything he imagined his life would be had changed. He was happy, despite the fact it was not what he had planned for his life.

It had been the highlight of his career when he'd been promoted to detective in the homicide division ten years ago. Unfortunately, that is when his life with Patty and the kids began to deteriorate. His work had become his passion and Patty and the kids had suffered as a result.

Bellamy gazed out the window of the cab and sighed miserably. If only he could go back in time and do it over, maybe things would be different. His gaze drifted up to the bleak, gray sky. The rain didn't show any signs of letting up, it reminded him of his own bleak life.

The cab window was being splattered with raindrops and it was a mere sixty two degrees in Seattle. That was a stark contrast to the eighty eight degrees he had left behind in Chicago. After much contemplation, he decided that Paloma must have left her home in Chicago for love as well. She was beautiful and successful, why else would she possibly come here? She had trained in Boston, surely

Boston had Seattle all beat to hell!

Bellamy arrived in his hotel room and unpacked. He picked up the phone and tried both of Paloma's numbers, but there was still no answer. He was beginning to wonder if she was screening her calls and just ignoring him. He went down to the hotel bar and had a beer, sighing and wondering why he had even come here. He looked around at all the laughing faces in the bar and wondered...if Marielle Benoit were in here in this bar, would he even recognize her? It was entirely possible she had changed her appearance. He frowned, if she wanted to make herself invisible to the police she could, he realized she wasn't stupid.

He pulled a crumpled piece of paper out of his pocket and decided he would go out to Paloma's house and have a look around.

He went to the hotel concierge who summoned a cab for him. The driver was a chatty Asian man, who was very nice at first, but was rapidly becoming annoying. The man took him to the ferry and in just a little over thirty minutes they had arrived on Bainbridge Island. The cab driver took him to Paloma's address, all the while telling Bellamy how rich these people were to be able to afford the beautiful houses here on the island. Bellamy couldn't really disagree with that, though if he was a multi millionaire, he doubted he'd be spending any of his money on a house anywhere in Seattle.

He told the driver to wait for him, then he walked up to the front door and rang the bell. After a few minutes, when he heard no stirring inside the house, he began to nose around. The house was locked up tight and boasted a security system. Bellamy sighed, he really didn't want to stir up the local PD by setting off the alarm. The drapes were drawn on all the first floor windows and he couldn't really see a thing. He was peeking through the glass of the back door when finally, he was startled by a voice.

"Can I help you?" asked the stout woman, who was standing there staring at him with wide brown eyes.

"I'm Detective Bellamy with the Chicago Police," he said, flashing his badge at her.

"Chicago police? Are you here about Mrs. Webster's mother?" cried the woman.

"I'm sorry, who are you?" asked Bellamy, eyeing the woman cautiously.

"I am Carmelita. I take care of the children and clean the house. I have heard that Mrs. Webster's mother was murdered and it was very disturbing to all of us. Did you catch the horrible person that did it?" cried the woman, her voice was breaking and she was tearing up.

"No, not yet. I have come here because I fear for Mrs. Webster's safety, we have reason to believe that she will be the murderer's next target. Can you tell me where she is?" asked Bellamy.

"Oh sweet Jesus have mercy on us," cried the woman,

pulling a rosary out of her pocket and kissing it. She paused to take a deep breath, her large brown eyes searching Bellamy's.

"Can you tell me where Mrs. Webster is?" asked Bellamy, he was beginning to lose his patience. Did no one realize? If Marielle got to Paloma first, the consequences would be deadly.

"Despite their strained relationship, Mrs. Webster has been very upset about her mother's death. The thought that someone had come into their house and murdered her mother had poor Mrs. Webster completely shaken up. Mr. Webster arranged for them to go away to Victoria for a week. The family loves it there," said Carmelita.

"Victoria...in Canada?" asked Bellamy.

"Yes, you can take the ferry. It's a beautiful town. Mrs. Webster loves to spend time there, she says it reminds her of Europe," said Carmelita.

"Can you tell me where they are staying?" asked Bellamy.

"Yes, they are staying at the Fairmont Empress, it's where they always stay," said Carmelita.

"Thank you," said Bellamy, turning and running back toward his cab. He needed to get to Paloma before Marielle figured out where she was.

He jogged anxiously back to his cab but the driver told him it was too late to get a ferry to Victoria, he would have to wait until tomorrow. He headed back to the hotel feeling defeated. He tried to look on the bright side, the slight delay would give him time to check in with headquarters. If they were lucky, Marielle had already been apprehended as she made her way toward Seattle.

Unfortunately, luck wasn't on their side. Bellamy called and talked to Salazar but he wasn't happy with the report. So far, law enforcement had flooded the I-90 corridor, but to no avail. There had been no sign of Marielle or her rented black Toyota Camry.

Bellamy sighed miserably. They knew what car she was in and they knew where she was headed, it shouldn't be that hard.

"What about the back roads? Is there a chance that she got off the interstate and started taking back roads to get to Seattle?"

"There's always a chance but she doesn't know her way around, so I seriously doubt she's done that. The interstate would be the most direct route," said Salazar.

"Apparently she is not that stupid. You do realize it is possible she could have bought a map or a GPS!" cried Bellamy, beginning to get irritated. "You do realize, if she gets to Paloma, she will kill her!" cried Bellamy.

"We're doing the best we can here, we've alerted law enforcement in Montana, Idaho and Washington to be on the lookout. What else can we do?" cried Salazar, he was frustrated that he was stuck there in Chicago, he wanted to be with Bellamy in the heart of things.

"Call me if you get anything," snapped Bellamy, snapping his cell phone shut, disgustedly. They had to find Marielle, he couldn't let her kill one more innocent person.

Chapter 19

Marielle climbed wearily back into her car, she was rueing her decision to take the back roads. It seemed as if it was taking forever. Unfortunately, she couldn't take any chances. By now, every law enforcement agency in the US would be on the lookout for her and her rented, black Toyota Camry.

She had been on the road for almost thirty six hours and was very near the Montana border finally. There was no time to rest though, she still had more than four hundred miles to cover before she would arrive in Seattle. She was now somewhere in rural western Montana, she would only have to cross the short tail of Idaho then she would finally be in Washington, though she needed to cross the entire state to get to Seattle. Flying would have been much faster but unfortunately, it was not an option.

Marielle had diverted her trip to the back roads. Unfortunately, she had run out of cash, so she had been forced to use her credit card in Billings Montana. She was well aware that the police could easily track her by her credit card use. She was certain they knew she was in Montana at least, and that was so much more than she wanted the police to know at this point.

She had bought an atlas and promptly abandoned the route she had originally planned on the interstate 90. She knew she would have to stay off the interstates from now on. She had no doubt that her parents bodies had been discovered in Mont Legun by now. In today's world of electronic connections, she assumed the authorities would have made the connection to her by now.

Marielle arrived in the small Montana town of Libby, which was definitely off the beaten path. She had really only traveled to large cities when she'd been in the states. She had only eaten in big city restaurants, she was thrown off by this small town, which seemed to be a collection of run down and mismatched buildings. As she drove through the town looking for a place to have lunch, it seemed as if nearly every business was closed up and had a for sale sign posted out front.

Finally, she found a small diner with a packed parking lot and decided this was where she would have lunch. A few old timers stared at her as she walked confidently into the diner. She was realizing she did look a bit out of place, everyone in the diner seemed to be dressed for camping or hiking, she was wearing a black sheath dress and heels.

She wasn't sure what to order, most of the food on the menu was foreign to her. She finally decided to ask the waitress for her recommendation for something light. She wanted a chance to try concealing her French accent. The waitress suggested the Cobb salad, and Marielle agreed, sincerely hoping that the plate wouldn't be covered with barren corn cobs when it arrived.

The salad turned out to be much better than she had

expected and the waitress didn't seem to suspect at all, that she was a murderer on the run from the police in a cross country chase. Marielle had to giggle to herself as she walked out of the restaurant to her car, thinking distractedly that she also needed to find a place to fill it with gas.

She had come so far already, but she still had many hours ahead before she arrived in Seattle. It was her blind rage that kept her going, she had already vowed that everyone who was responsible for her pain over the last forty six years would die. She had to make it to Paloma, even though she was so tired and achy she didn't think she could possibly last another minute in that car.

She wondered if the bodies of her adoptive parents had been found back in Mont Legun...surely they had. They had friends who would miss their presence about town. With Sabine being such a high profile personality, it wouldn't take the authorities long to put two and two together.

She chewed on her lower lip anxiously, she was now thinking it would be a good idea to somehow ditch the Camry, but she still had a lot of ground to cover. She knew it would be easy to steal a car in this small town. Though stealing a car would be a bad decision. If she stole a car that would be as bad as attaching a neon sign to herself. She shook her head miserably, she had to think of something else.

Marielle sighed and looked around in frustration, what could she possibly do? She smiled in delight when, just across the street she saw a worn brick building, a sign posted over the garage door that advertised "Bill Puryear-Mechanic", in red and white peeling paint.

Marielle smiled in satisfaction. Of course, this was small town USA, if she were to have car trouble surely they would loan a car to a poor, helpless woman.

She was almost giggling in anticipation as she pulled the large hunting knife she had bought in Illinois out of her purse. She went to the front of the car, opened the hood and sliced through the serpentine belt with ease. Then she grabbed her purse, placed the knife back inside and walked across the street to the garage.

She looked totally out of place there, in rural Montana. She had attracted plenty of stares in the restaurant where most of the patrons were locals and tourists who came to enjoy the river and camping in the mountains and were dressed for such.

Marielle looked stunning for a woman of forty six years old. She was wearing a black silk dress, black stilettos and her pale blond hair was pulled up in an elegant chignon. It was how she dressed all the time in Paris but in Libby Montana, she stood out like a sore thumb.

She worried that everyone in the entire US was looking for her, but she felt confident going to the garage. Chances are, this Bill Puryear didn't watch the World news. She would be able to conceal her accent enough if she concentrated, she wasn't worried.

"Excuse me?" she called, she had been working on an American southern accent for the past three hours, she had nothing else to do. She'd been trapped in the car, sometimes for hours at a time with only poor radio reception because of the mountains. Practicing an accent kept her mind off her anger. She almost giggled when she heard herself, it was actually pretty good!

"Hello Ma'am," said a man, from behind the greasy desk. The man was older, in his late fifties she was guessing. He was unshaven and wearing a grease stained flannel shirt and Carharts. Marielle fought the look of smug satisfaction that was threatening to wash across her face, this was perfect. The guy was a backwoods hick, he probably didn't even have electricity at his house!

"I was hoping you could help me, there's something wrong with my car," she said, smiling sweetly at him.

"Sure thing, let me take a look," he said, standing up to follow her out of the garage.

"It's right across the street, at the restaurant," said Marielle, trying desperately to conceal her delight. This guy was going to be a pushover and she was getting the feeling he didn't watch the news at all, which was good. She was almost sure that law enforcement had figured out who the prime suspect in Sabine Rousseau's murder was by now.

She'd cleaned up the crime scene well enough, she was sure she hadn't left behind any fingerprints or DNA, but she was almost certain that the bodies of her parents had been found by now. They had close friends who would miss their presence in town. The Gendarmerie Nationale would try to find her to question her in her parents murders, they would realize that she had left the country and flown to Chicago. Eventually, they would put two and two together, it really wouldn't be that hard.

Marielle smiled smugly. Yes, by now the Chicago police would be looking for her. Even complete morons would have figured everything out by now.

"I love your southern accent, are you from Alabama? I got family in Alabama," said the man, assessing her carefully.

"Atlanta, Georgia, actually," she said, smiling sweetly. It was actually the only Southern U.S. town that would come to her mind at the moment. She flashed him a slightly seductive smile, he smiled back, completely enchanted by her.

"Uh, huh," he murmured, seemingly at a loss for words.

The man followed her to the car and had her pop the hood, he checked everything over.

"Here's your problem sweetheart, your serpentine belt is toast," he said, showing it to her.

"Really, what's that?" she asked, shrugging and looking completely lost. The poor helpless woman routine worked every time on these older men, especially small town guys.

"It used to be that cars had all sorts of belts, now most of them just have this serpentine belt that controls almost everything, you won't get too far in this car," he said.

"Oh no! I have a job interview in Spokane tomorrow morning. What am I going to do?" cried Marielle, completely oozing helplessness.

"I can fix it, no problem, but I don't have this part in stock. They'll have to send me one up from Missoula, I could have her fixed by tomorrow afternoon," he told her, giving her a wry smile.

"Oh it will be too late, I can't reschedule this interview! I've left my poor mother at home with the neighbors, she's got cancer and she needs constant care. I was hoping to get this job, and bring her to live with me, I don't know how much time she has left," cried Marielle, breaking down in tears and milking it for everything it was worth.

"It's OK honey," he said, patting her on the shoulder, uneasily. "Ummm...if you'd be coming back this way in the next couple days I could loan you that little Ford Focus there. It's small, but she'll get you there, no problem," he said, pointing to the tiny car. Marielle gave the man a sweet smile, it took every ounce of concentration she had to avoid bursting out in maniacal laughter. It was too perfect, the man was basically giving her an escape car! They would never find her in the little blue car, they were all looking for the Camry.

"Would you really do that? That would be so kind! You are just like an angel from heaven, don't you worry I'll just be one day in Spokane and then I'll be back. You have no idea how much I appreciate this," cried Marielle, in her practiced southern accent. She surprised the man by throwing her arms around him in a hug.

The man helped Marielle move all her things into the little blue Ford including the small blue cooler that contained Sabine's heart, which was sitting unpretentiously on the back seat. Marielle breathed a sigh of relief that he hadn't peeked in.

Soon she was waving to the man and back on the road. She still had quite a few hours ahead of her, but she was free and clear. No one was looking for the little blue Focus with Montana license plates. She was so excited, she was almost considering cutting back down south to the interstate and taking that the rest of the way. She decided she would do that. It was a straight shot, it would cut her travel time down by several hours.

Marielle screamed in delight when she was finally on the interstate. She had managed to ditch the Camry and no one would be looking for her in the little Focus. It had been so easy, the man in the small town had no clue as to her true identity. He was convinced that she was a poor, innocent woman from Atlanta. She giggled at her own cunningness, now she was in a car that was virtually undetectable to the police. She could make it to Seattle without a worry.

Marielle settled in for her long drive. She had nothing but the radio and her own messed up mind to entertain her. She thought about all she had accomplished in the past several days and the final task that lay ahead of her in Seattle.

She was ecstatic, her mission was nearly accomplished, she had almost destroyed everyone in her life who had destroyed her. Paloma would be her final victory.

She almost snarled when she thought about Paloma. That bitch Paloma had stole her rightful life. Marielle shook her head miserably, it was all perfectly ridiculous. She was Sabine Rousseau's eldest daughter, she was the one with all the talent. Yet it had been Paloma who had won all the roles in the movies and the musicals, even though her talent was only marginal.

Marielle knew that she was the one, who had been blessed with the talent, she had been told that her entire life. She had even been compared to Sabine Rousseau years ago, when no one knew that she was actually Sabine's illegitimate daughter. Unfortunately, show business was a tough business. Growing up in Mont Legun had left Marielle at a severe disadvantage, she had never had an "in".

Her parents were just small town business people, they knew no one important. They lived comfortably, but they weren't rich. Nothing had ever been handed to Marielle, she had to fight for every single victory she had ever accomplished. She had grown up a no one, she never had the luxury or prestige of being Sabine's true daughter.

It wasn't fair, Paloma had basically been handed the life Marielle had wanted for herself on a silver platter, yet she never deserved it or appreciated it. She ran away from her life in the theater and disgraced her family with her shameless antics, running off with a French playboy when her own family had ensured her position in society by having her engaged to marry a respected British nobel.

She couldn't believe how stupid Paloma had been, Arthur Barrington was an Earl, much respected and very rich, but Paloma had run away from her family obligations, claiming instead to be in love with French hotelier Stephane Aubiere. The fall out from all the bad publicity had left the family seriously damaged.

Marielle was still angry, she had been scammed, she had gone through her entire life believing that Jean Paul and Claudine were her real parents. For more than forty six years, they never thought to tell her that Jean Paul her father, was nothing but a sex starved womanizer.

They never thought to tell her that on her holiday to Paris, Sabine Rousseau had spent many nights out at clubs dancing with the ballet company's handsome accountant. They never told her that Sabine had ended many nights in Paris in Jean Paul's bed. When she came down from her alcohol and cocaine induced euphoria she would slink back to her own apartment in shame.

Unfortunately, they had been careless during the course of their torrid affair. Sabine had been horrified to learn that she had inadvertently gotten pregnant, when she was already engaged to marry wealthy film mogul Harvey

Bernard who at the time, was on location filming a movie in the heart of China.

Sabine had been panicked when she had found out she was pregnant. There was no way she could convince Harvey the baby was his, he'd been gone for too many weeks. Sabine had no interest in keeping the baby or settling down with someone so bourgeois as Jean Paul Benoit.

Though Jean Paul had begged her relentlessly, Sabine Rousseau would never give up her engagement to the great Harvey Bernard. Though he was much older than her, he was wealthy and famous, a perfect husband as far as Sabine was concerned. She felt she was royalty compared to Jean Paul and despite his pleas, she refused to keep the baby, so Jean Paul himself agreed to adopt her.

Even though their affair was brief, Jean Paul had fallen deeply in love with Sabine, he would have done anything for Sabine, to convince her to spend the rest of her life with him. But it was not meant to be, Sabine felt she was much too good to spend the rest of her life with a lowly French accountant of very moderate means.

Jean Paul was heartbroken by Sabine's refusal, but what could he do? He himself, was already married to Claudine, who would never have a baby of her own. Their loveless marriage would never be blessed with a child, despite the constant nagging from both sides of the family. At Jean Paul's urging, Claudine agreed to adopt the baby. It seemed like a good plan at the time. The grandparents would get the grand baby they had been harping for and Claudine would not have to spend any time in Jean Paul's bed to get it.

What Claudine did not realize was that Jean Paul's obsession with Sabine Rousseau was so all consuming, he would ruin his own daughter's childhood.

Marielle's early childhood had been uneventful for the most part. Jean Paul had kept himself busy with his work in Paris and had been mainly absent from her life. He had his work with the Paris Ballet and most evenings he still frequented clubs, often hooking up with random women.

Claudine stayed in Mont Legun, ran their quaint bed and breakfast and played the part of Marielle's loving mother. To the outside world, they had the perfect little family. No one in the town of Mont Legun even suspected that Marielle was adopted. Of course, she had her father's nose.

Claudine cared for Marielle. She kept her fed and clothed, but as a mother she was distant and affection less. Marielle's entire life consisted of her ballet classes three days a week, and of course, school where she was a bright and engaging student.

Marielle's life suddenly changed one night when she was just seven years old. Claudine had gone into town for the evening and Jean Paul asked Marielle to come into his bedroom. He told her he had a present for her. Marielle never really got presents, so she was excited when her father presented her with a tiny silver cross on a chain. She almost cried when she saw the delicate filigree cross, it was the most beautiful thing she had ever seen!

Marielle threw her arms around him and hugged him, she had never been given a gift so beautiful, ever! The Benoit family lived a comfortable enough life, but Jean Paul shunned spending money on jewelry and fancy trinkets. He believed in spending money on books and education.

Marielle had been so excited with her father's gift, she jumped into her father's arms and hugged him, she gave him a kiss on the cheek. Her father squeezed her tightly and pulled her onto his lap, something he hadn't done since she was a toddler. Then he kissed her.

Jean Paul held her tightly in his arms and kissed her on both cheeks repeatedly. Marielle was in heaven. In her entire life, neither of her parents had shown her any affection and she was starved for it.

In moments her father was trailing kisses down her neck. Marielle wrapped her arms around him tighter, completely overwhelmed by the feelings of love. Then her father took her face in his hands and began kissing her on the lips. Marielle, was kissing him back...till he suddenly plunged his tongue into her mouth.

Marielle was suddenly confused and trying to pull away. No one had ever kissed her like that! Her father pulled her firmly back onto his lap and kept kissing her. Marielle was suddenly frightened as her father's big hands held her down and the kisses grew more intense. His hands were suddenly roaming across her body and she was suddenly feeling very uncomfortable.

"Pappa, what are you doing?" she cried, trying to pull herself from his arms. He had never touched her like that before. She was just a little girl, but her sixth sense was telling her that this was just wrong.

Jean Paul smiled at her and told her that he loved her very much. He gave her a very serious look and told her if she loved him also, she would stay there in his bedroom and let him prove to her how much he loved her.

Marielle was still nervous, but she had been told she should never disobey her father, so she just nodded. Neither of her parents had ever shown her any affection. She craved it. Her father was a very smart and respected man, so she was sure that he knew what he was talking about.

When her father plunged his tongue into her mouth, she let him. When he pressed his body against hers, she knew that he loved her, so she let him. Even when his hands seemed to travel to places she knew they shouldn't, she said nothing. He was her father, he loved her...

Marielle was frightened when her father started to take her clothes off, she was sure he hadn't seen her naked since she was just a baby. But if her own papa told her it was OK, then what could she do? She could not question him, she was just a little girl, he was the adult.

Marielle could not comprehend the strange things he

was doing to her, it seemed very wrong. She cried and cried when he did that to her, at first it hurt...really bad.

He told her she should not be scared, what they were doing was special. He told her that he just loved her more than most papas did so she was lucky. He told her that they had a special love and she should not tell anyone or they would both get into trouble. He told her that other people would be jealous of their special love, especially her mother.

When Marielle finally returned to her own room that night, she cried herself to sleep. She shuddered when she thought about her father's sweaty body on top of her, hurting her. She cried and cried when she thought about the awful things he did to her.

Years passed by and Marielle kept busy with school and her now daily classes at the ballet school in the village. Still, she began to realize, whenever Claudine would leave the house, her father would ask her to come to his bedroom and she would get special love. At first she didn't like it, it seemed creepy and unnatural, though her life was so devoid of the affection she craved, soon she began to look forward to the special love her father gave her.

Claudine her adopted mother, had never given her any sort of affection her entire life. Yes, she took care of her, but it was obvious to Marielle that her own mother did not love her. In fact, as the years went on, their relationship seemed to grow more and more strained.

Claudine desired order and perfection above all, if

Marielle left a mess, broke a dish or got a poor grade, Claudine would punish her by beating her violently and calling her horrible names that Marielle didn't understand. She would go to her bedroom and cry for her Papa, who was usually out of town at the time. Then later, Marielle was forced to hide the bruises with long sleeves and pants, even in the summer time.

On the opposite end of the spectrum was her relationship with her father. Her father would hold her in his arms in his bed and tell her how much he loved her, while Claudine became more and more distant.

Her adoptive mother Claudine, was generally unhappy in life. She knew and respected her obligations. Her family had been ecstatic that she had married Jean Paul and the two of them had a lovely daughter, but she herself, was not happy with her life.

Claudine was a good cook, kept their house spotless and ran their little bed and breakfast with ease. Unfortunately, her marriage to Jean Paul seemed to be passionless. Whenever he would kiss her, she would push him away. Then she would conveniently leave the cottage so that Jean Paul could have his way with his daughter. Marielle was sure that she knew...

Marielle could never forgive her birth mother. Sabine had left her own daughter behind in France and let her be adopted, just so she could return to the states and marry a man she believed was more sophisticated than the womanizing accountant she'd had an affair with in France.

She wondered how Sabine could so callously leave her own daughter behind with her true father. This man worshipped Sabine so much, he decided one day that Marielle had become Sabine and he spent the next nearly ten years, fantasizing that he was making love to Sabine, when truly, he was committing incest with his own daughter. It all ended when she was seventeen...

Then there was Paloma, beautiful, talented Paloma. Everyone loved Paloma, she was America's little darling. She appeared in her first movie when she was just six, just about the same time Jean Paul had decided that Marielle looked so much like Sabine, he couldn't take it anymore, and he started taking Marielle into his bedroom.

Yes, Paloma had seen her share of tragedy, her beloved fiancee was killed in the accident that had nearly killed Paloma too. Everyone said it was a miracle that she survived...but she was strong. Anyone related to Sabine had to be strong. Sabine would never just lay down and die.

Marielle was strong too. She had survived all those years being taken to her own father's bedroom. She had rationalized it as special love...she actually felt bad for all those other girls who's papas didn't give them special love. Yes, she was strong, she had survived a pregnancy and an illegal abortion that nearly killed her when she was seventeen.

Marielle had known right away she was pregnant, she

also knew her father would never let her keep their baby. She had never even had a boyfriend, but she wanted this baby she had conceived with her father...it was special.

She concealed her pregnancy as long as she could, but of course he realized when he took her into his bedroom. Her abdomen was swelling, her breasts were getting larger, her nipples were tender. Her father was angry with her for not telling him. He told her they had to abort the baby, it would be a monster if they allowed it to continue to grow in her womb.

Marielle argued with him and cried, but still, he insisted that he take her to Paris for an abortion. Marielle had concealed her pregnancy for so long, she was much further along than anyone realized.

She had cried and cried when she woke up in the clinic and saw the surgical table strewn with the mangled body parts of her baby, the baby her father would not allow her to have.

When she had finally recovered from her ordeal, her father told her she had to leave their house. He told her she looked too much like a woman he had loved, he couldn't stand to have Marielle in his home anymore.

Marielle was hurt, her father had told her he would love her forever, he told her he would never want anyone else as much as he wanted her, but it had all been a fantasy. He had come to his senses, he knew that keeping Marielle around who was now fully developed and looked eerily like

Sabine, would be a bad idea.

Poor Marielle was young and naive, she didn't know what to do. She had foolishly thought that her father loved her in a special way and he would never abandon her. He gave her five hundred dollars and told her she should go to Paris and dance because dancing was in her blood.

Marielle was completely lost. She had studied ballet since she had been four years old. She had always been the best in her school, but she didn't see how she could just run off to Paris and somehow find a job. It was all very overwhelming...

Chapter 20

Bellamy looked out across the water. It was nine a.m. and he was on the ferry, on his way to Victoria British Columbia. Once again, the weather left a little something to be desired. It was gray and rainy again.

He'd been trying without success, to contact Paloma. He'd called her on her cell and at the hotel multiple times. He really wanted to put her on guard that her life might be in danger, but Paloma was apparently serious about her privacy, even the hotel staff refused to bother her.

Bellamy had spoke with his office this morning, they had informed him that no one had apprehended Marielle as of yet. He couldn't help but wonder why they couldn't seem to find her. How hard could it be to find a black Toyota Camry, when every law enforcement agency in the country knew it's destination and was looking for it? Bellamy was angry, he would not allow Paloma to be Marielle's last victim. He really just wanted to get to Paloma and get her somewhere safe until Marielle was apprehended.

Finally, the ferry was docked and Bellamy was relieved he had finally arrived in Victoria. On questioning a man on the dock, he was happy to find out the hotel was within walking distance and the weather seemed to be clearing a bit, he could see the sun peeking through the clouds. Hopefully a sign that things were getting better, he thought to himself.

He headed through the crowded marina area and could see the majestic hotel was not far away. In minutes he arrived at the front desk of the opulent hotel, the woman standing there smiled at him.

"Can I help you?" she asked.

"Yes, my name is Detective Bellamy, I'm with the Chicago Police. It is imperative that I get in touch with Dr. Paloma Webster, I understand she is staying here," he said.

"I'm very sorry sir, I'm afraid you've just missed her. The family left by seaplane about an hour ago," said the woman.

"Are you certain? I was told they were here for a week," said Bellamy, sighing in frustration.

"They were booked for a week, but their six year old daughter was quite ill with an ear infection. She apparently cried all night last night for her nanny "Litty", Mr. Webster said they couldn't take it anymore and they were taking her home," said the woman with a shrug.

"Thank you," said Bellamy, turning to leave. He hesitated before he walked out, taking a seaplane would be much faster than waiting to take the ferry back.

"How can I get a seaplane flight?" he asked, turning back around and approaching the woman.

"I can arrange it for you," she told him with a smile.

In less than half an hour he was standing on the dock waiting to board the seaplane. Bellamy was a little anxious, he'd flown a lot in his life, but this was by far, the smallest plane he had ever flown on.

He had to admit, the take off was bumpier and scarier than any flight he had ever been on, but once they were in the air he was able to relax and enjoy the scenery. When he arrived in Seattle he called headquarters again to check and see if Marielle had been apprehended yet. Unfortunately, the answer was no.

No one had seen her Black Toyota Camry on I-90, or any back roads so far. It seemed as if Marielle Benoit had disappeared into thin air. Bellamy was worried, enough time had elapsed now she was most likely in Seattle, possibly stalking her target right now. Salazar told him to relax, he had contacted the Seattle PD and they had sent some uniformed officers out to her house, they were going to take her and her family someplace safe.

Bellamy wondered, was anyplace really safe?

Chapter 21

Marielle felt a little bit better, she had taken a short nap during the ferry ride, now she was driving down the streets of Bainbridge Island looking for the address that would allow her to finish her mission.

Today would end her forty six years of pain. Pain caused by a birth mother that didn't want her, an adoptive mother who never really cared for her, and a father who she had loved dearly, who she had believed loved her above everyone else. Her father had taken away her innocence, used her, and then threw her carelessly into the gutter.

Her own father's sick, twisted fantasies had completely destroyed her childhood and even worse than that, they had left her completely unable to have a real relationship with any man. She had been betrayed and lied to her entire life.

Now her attention was focused on Paloma. It just wasn't right. Paloma had lived the very life that should have been hers. Marielle shook her head miserably, that bitch Paloma had it all and she didn't even appreciate it.

Sabine hadn't cast Paloma away. Of course, she was the legitimate child of Sabine and her high society husband, movie mogul Harvey Bernard. Harvey was about fourteen years older than Sabine and he had completely adored Sabine and their three children.

Paloma had grown up in the limelight. She was beautiful, but as far as Marielle was concerned, only a mediocre dancer. Still, she had been handed movie and musical roles as if they were candy, and of course, she was beautiful and highly sought after by men.

Marielle had followed Paloma's controversial life before she had even realized the connection they had. Marielle had admired Sabine's dancing since she had been a child. Anytime Sabine had been a guest of the Paris Ballet, her father would take her to Paris so they could see the ballet. Her father told her some day she would be a prima ballerina, just like Sabine.

It was later that Marielle became obsessed with Sabine's daughter Paloma. They were close in age, and looked remarkably alike. Marielle was just a year older and when she went to the ballet with her father, she was sometimes mistaken for Paloma, the resemblance was so striking. This delighted Marielle, but seemed to anger her father, who would get angry and call Paloma awful names, names so awful Marielle was ashamed to repeat them.

Marielle never knew why her father seemed to hate Sabine Rousseau's daughter so badly, but he seemed to worship Sabine. He would plan their trips to Paris for months ahead of time. Her mother Claudine always refused to go with them, she had her quilting club and she hated to travel.

It wasn't until that fateful day when her parents had finally told her the truth about her childhood, that everything finally seemed to make sense.

Marielle was in shock when they told her that Sabine Rousseau was her birth mother. Her parents told her that Sabine had an affair with Jean Paul, who even after all these years, had never gotten over her. Their love affair had been passionate, but in the end Sabine had dumped him, because he was a nobody.

Jean Paul was miserable with his life. He had married Claudine Fortescue when he was very young. The Benoits and the Fortescues were very close, it was expected that Jean Paul marry Claudine, they had nearly grown up together. Claudine was attractive enough, Jean Paul thought their children would be attractive also.

Unfortunately, his marriage had been nothing but a one night stand. When Jean Paul woke up on his first morning as a married man, his new wife brought him breakfast in bed and announced that she hoped with all her heart that he had gotten her pregnant that night, because she detested his touch and there was no way she would ever allow him to do that to her again, ever!

For some reason they stayed married, their relationship a marriage of convenience. Their families were so happy with the union, neither one could bare to tell them the sad truth. Their relationship had been consummated that one time and there would never be any children from Claudine's womb.

After that first night, Claudine never allowed Jean Paul into her bed again. She knew he had affairs, she realized he had needs, she didn't care where he went to fulfill those needs, as long as he didn't come to her.

Claudine had no interest in Jean Paul's affection or his lovemaking, she had her own life, most nights she went to her quilting club, or that is what Marielle had always believed. It wasn't until she was an adult, that she realized her mother's quilting club was merely a cover up for her mother's lesbian lifestyle.

Theirs was a family destined for self destruction. Marielle had cried so many tears in her life, she had vowed to shed no more. She had endured secret beatings from a mother who hated her very existence. She endured more than ten years of incest at the hands of her father. Then, at the time of her life when she was most vulnerable, he had her baby aborted, then he heartlessly kicked her out of the house.

Marielle had nightmares for years of the baby that was ripped from her womb. She could still see it as it laid dismembered on the cold, sterile operating room table. She woke up in the dingy room racked with pain, her mind still fuzzy from the drugs. When she saw her baby's body there on the table, bloody and torn to pieces she started crying. The doctor gazed at her callously and snapped at her.

"That's what happens when little sluts cannot keep their legs closed."

"I am not a slut," cried Marielle. "He loves me, the baby was abnormal, that is why I did it."

"There was nothing wrong with your baby, it was fine. You were a selfish slut, you had it murdered, so you can have more trysts," said the doctor, eyeing her arrogantly and walking out of the room.

Marielle cried all the way home to Mont Legun. How could the baby have been fine when her father told her it would be abnormal, a monster? She had wanted this baby with all her heart...why?

"Papa, the doctor told me I murdered my baby," wailed Marielle.

"We did it child, we made a choice to take the baby's life, may God forgive us," said Jean Paul.

"I wanted my baby...you told me..."

"You will shut up right now. I will hear no more talk of this baby. It is a sin...it would be wrong, you could never keep the baby. You are almost eighteen now, do you not realize it is a sin to have relations with your own father?" cried Jean Paul.

"I wasn't my fault, you told me the love we have is special," cried Marielle.

"You seduced me. I could not resist, I was evil and full of lust. I should have not done such a thing with my own daughter, it was a sin, the lust hath took over my body, I was not rational. You will go to the priest and confess your sins. I cannot...I am too evil," said Jean Paul.

"No papa, you are not evil, you love me. The love we have is special," said Marielle, sobbing miserably.

"You will do as I tell you. You will confess your sins and be forgiven. I have buried my evil seed deep inside of you, but we have been given a second chance. The doctor has removed the demon child from your womb. You will start anew, never again should you feel me inside you...it is wrong. You will go to the priest and be forgiven," said Jean Paul, he was sobbing now.

"But I love you papa, I want your baby growing inside of me! It is our baby, I long for it," cried Marielle, miserably. She had listened to his lies for so long, she no longer knew the difference between wrong and right.

"God be my witness, I am sorry for what I did. Dear Marielle, I fear I have ruined you, you know not what is good any more. I could not help it, I swear. May God have mercy on my soul," said Jean Paul, who now appeared to be praying to God.

Her father took her to church that day and she prayed, she prayed for her baby and she prayed for her father, but she refused to confess her sins and be forgiven, she could never be forgiven for what she had done...

Chapter 22

Bellamy arrived back on Bainbridge Island hoping that the uniforms were already there with Paloma. As he pulled into the driveway he saw that there were two police cars in the driveway. He breathed a silent sigh of relief, there was no way that Marielle could get to Paloma now. He jogged up the front steps of the house and rang the bell.

Carmelita opened the door and showed him into the living room where there were four police officers, two children and a tall man in a dark colored suit who Bellamy assumed must be Drake Webster. Bellamy looked around the room anxiously, where was Paloma?

"Detective Bellamy of the Chicago Police Department," said Carmelita, introducing him to everyone in the room.

"Drake Webster," said the tall man in the suit as he approached Bellamy and offered him his hand to shake.

Bellamy shook the man's hand, looking him over carefully. He was tall and attractive and he seemed to be a bit nervous.

"Nice to meet you Mr. Webster," said Bellamy, shaking his hand firmly.

"I have to admit, I was a bit confused when all the police showed up at the house. I don't understand why this French woman may be after Paloma. I can't imagine that the two have ever met," said Drake, shaking his head in confusion.

"They are essentially half sisters and no, I don't think that fate has ever brought them together. The danger, I believe, is all in Marielle's head. Marielle, who is also Sabine's daughter, grew up in France leading a less than privileged life. Paloma, on the other hand, grew up in a mansion living her life in the spotlight as the daughter of Sabine and her husband Harvey Bernard."

"Fame and fortune may seem glamorous from the outside. Marielle, had no idea, I'm sure, of the obstacles Paloma has had to overcome. In Marielle's eyes, Paloma had the perfect life...a life that should have been hers," said Bellamy.

Drake was staring at him, as he suddenly comprehended how dangerous Marielle truly was.

"Do you believe she can make it all the way to Seattle?" asked Drake.

"I believe she is already here. Where is Paloma?" asked Bellamy, glancing around the room at all the anxious faces staring at him.

"She has gone to the hospital to check on a patient she has been very worried about. It is an eight year old girl with cancer, she is quite ill. She felt very bad about going out of town when this little girl's death was quite imminent," said Drake.

"They let her go to the hospital?" cried Bellamy, flashing an accusing glare at the four uniformed police in the room.

He was thoroughly enraged, were they completely mad? Marielle Benoit was out there just waiting for them to screw up and they had done it. There was no way, even with a police escort, that Paloma could be safe at the hospital. It was too crowded, too open...

"Just relax there cowboy, she's got an escort with her," snapped a female officer, rolling her eyes in boredom.

"And you are?"

"Officer Pennington," said the woman, assessing him nonchalantly.

"I'm not sure why your department hasn't moved this entire family to a "safe house" when my department has already briefed you on the danger of this situation. Who's your supervisor?" asked Bellamy, his face was red and he was obviously distressed by the situation. His heart was contorted in fear for Paloma, who probably had no idea how much danger she was in.

"Don't you think you're overreacting a little bit, Detective Bellamy. This house has a first class security system and truly, you have no proof that your suspect is really after Mrs. Webster. In fact, no one has even seen this woman since she was in Billings Montana. She's off the map, she's in hiding. Do you really believe not going to drive her ass all the way to Seattle over a half sister she's never even met?" snapped Officer Pennington, shaking her head miserably.

"This woman is psychotic and she's already murdered

three people. I have no idea how she has managed to slip past every law enforcement agency in the western United States, but mark my words, she is here and Paloma Webster is in danger," snapped Bellamy, staring the woman down arrogantly.

"If she were anywhere in Seattle, we'd have her in custody already, I think you're freaking out over nothing," said Pennington, still rolling her eyes miserably.

"If you had seen the body in our morgue, you would realize that I am not freaking out about nothing. This woman is dangerous, and I would advise that you call your escort with Mrs. Webster and make sure that they are on top of their game. I wouldn't be surprised if Ms. Benoit has her eyes on Paloma Webster right now," said Bellamy.

He looked around the room slowly. Everyone else seemed to be stunned into silence. Mr. Webster looked distraught, his six year old daughter had crawled into his arms and he was just standing there numbly as she whined annoyingly into his ear. The other three officers in the room had been stunned into speechlessness and Carmelita was anxiously stroking her rosary. Bellamy suddenly felt the overwhelming need to get to Paloma himself. He couldn't shake the feeling that Marielle was already here, planning her attack. The danger was almost palpable to him.

"Where can I find Doctor Webster?" he asked.

"She's at Seattle Children's hospital," sputtered Drake, still trying uselessly, to quiet his whining child.

"Thank you, I'll be in touch," said Bellamy, giving him a brief nod and heading for the door.

He let himself out the front door and climbed into his car. He was disappointed, the Seattle police didn't seem to be taking any of this very seriously. He would have to go to the hospital himself and retrieve Paloma. He didn't feel safe having her out in public until Marielle was apprehended.

He was prepared to back out of the driveway when his cell phone started jangling in his pocket.

"Bellamy," he grunted impatiently.

"Doug, it's me Penny. I have some very disturbing news to tell you."

"Hit me," said Bellamy, his heart faltered, he was almost afraid to hear what the disturbing news was. His first thought was that Marielle had already got to Paloma, it made his heart race nervously.

"The Toyota Camry has been found," said Penny, though her voice was not overjoyed at the news.

"Excellent, so Marielle can't be far. That's great," said Bellamy, relief suddenly flooding his body.

"No, it's not great." said Penny. "The car was found at a mechanic's shop in Libby Montana. According to the sheriff's department, the mechanic there loaned Marielle a car two days ago."

"Holy shit, we've been looking for the wrong car!" cried Bellamy, rolling his eyes miserably.

"She's in a blue Ford Focus, Montana license plate

number Adam, one, seven, six, nine, nine," said Penny.

"Got it," said Bellamy, jotting it on his notepad.

He pulled out of the driveway and headed toward the hospital. He could only hope he wasn't too late.

Chapter 23

Marielle pulled her car up on a little rise that overlooked the Webster's house. As she looked down at the house below her she frowned, she was too late. There were three police cars in the driveway. Her heart sank with a troubling realization. The police had figured out that Paloma was in danger, her plan was foiled! She'd hoped to break into Paloma's house tonight and kill her while she slept. Though she really wanted to confront Paloma and tell her every hellish nightmare that defined her very life.

She knew that was impossible though, she had decided that killing Paloma in her sleep was the only way. Once people knew you were angry and wanted them dead, they always fought back. It only made things harder and messier. It was just as satisfying to murder them in their sleep, like she had Jean Paul and Claudine. Those two fools had never seen it coming. She had slit their throats first, essentially silencing them, then she was able to exact her revenge.

No, it wasn't necessary for her victim to be awake, though it had been very satisfying to see the terrified look in her birth mother's eyes when she plunged the knife into her chest. Sabine realized, at that moment, that she wasn't as all powerful as she'd imagined she was. She was about to die, and there was absolutely nothing she could do about it. Marielle giggled a satisfied giggle at the very thought. Sabine had thought she was invincible, a goddess of sorts, she had gotten exactly what she deserved.

Marielle thought back to the first time she had contacted Sabine on the phone. She explained to Sabine who she was and what her parents had finally confessed to her. At first, Sabine denied everything. She called her a complete nut case and told her never to contact her again, she wanted nothing to do with her. This of course, had completely enraged her.

Marielle refused to give up, Sabine was her birth mother. She merely wanted to be acknowledged, so the phone calls continued. As time went on, Sabine seemed to be softening a bit, resigned to the fact that the jig was up, and her illegitimate daughter knew the truth. During one of their many phone calls Sabine told Marielle she had been scared when she found out she was pregnant, it had been a careless mistake.

She was already engaged to marry Hollywood legend Harvey Bernard, who was away in China for many weeks filming a movie. Sabine worried if Harvey had found out that she had bore an illegitimate child, he would never want to marry her. Marielle had rolled her eyes miserably when she heard that excuse. Of course, it was always about what was best for Sabine. What about her, the baby she had left behind?

Marielle had felt so lost her entire life, she just wanted

to believe that her existence in life was a product of love. In her whole life she had never felt secure. Her own family had been so distant and loveless, their little family unit had been a complete sham. Unfortunately, the story Sabine told her was not what she wanted to hear and it broke her heart.

When Marielle spoke to Sabine on the phone, she implored Sabine to tell her all about the love affair she had with Jean Paul. Jean Paul had been so in love with Sabine, Marielle couldn't wait to hear Sabine's side of the story, she was so sure that it was a beautiful romantic story of true love that could never be realized.

Marielle knew that Jean Paul had already been married to Claudine, so Marielle truly believed that it had been unfortunate circumstances that had kept them apart. She believed that Sabine had longed for him, as much as he had longed for her. Sabine, being true to form, did not offer up the warm and fuzzy story that Marielle had been craving.

She told Marielle that she had never been in love with Jean Paul. It was the sixties, they were players, they both liked to hit the clubs and dance all night. They had both lived the fast lifestyle in Paris, sex, drugs, alcohol. Sabine explained that during most of her affair with Jean Paul she had been existing in a drug and alcohol induced haze.

Her evenings consisted of champagne, cocaine and sex. Sabine had further ruined the story by telling Marielle that Jean Paul wasn't the only man she had slept with during those weeks. She'd not only had multiple lovers, but the cocaine had removed her inhibitions to the point that she had found herself involved in several orgies. Sabine explained that she couldn't remember for sure. Marielle was completely horrified by Sabine's story.

Sabine explained that she was usually very careful, she had no desire to get pregnant. Being a famous dancer, it would ruin her career. Unfortunately, she had fallen easily into the party scene. There had been lots of champagne and apparently lots of cocaine too, so her diaphragm, which she used religiously, had been all but forgotten.

Sabine claimed that she barely remembered some of those nights, though it had been Jean Paul's bed that she usually woke up in. He of course was head over heels in love with her and always made sure he brought her home from the parties. Unfortunately, Sabine wasn't looking for a relationship. She was already engaged to Harvey, who would be furious if he knew she had been sleeping her way around Paris. Jean Paul continued to pursue her long after she had slunk away in shame those mornings she woke up, not able to remember what had happened the night before. Though she couldn't remember much, she knew what her life had become. Sabine admitted to Marielle that she had been completely out of control, she could not confirm or deny that Jean Paul was her true father.

Marielle was heartbroken and angry that her birth mother was such a tramp, she couldn't even confirm that Jean Paul was her real father, though Marielle had always known that he was...she had his nose.

Marielle continued to converse with Sabine occasionally, it eventually seemed as if Sabine was finally accepting her, which made Marielle very happy. She planned to fly to Chicago and meet Sabine, she was anxious to meet the rest of her family too. She was excited to finally have a real family, a birth mother, a half brother and two half sisters. She'd never had siblings growing up, and she was very excited to have some now. Sabine burst her fragile bubble when she told her that she would never publicly accept her, a meeting between the entire family was never going to happen.

Marielle was stunned, for the first time in her life, she had finally felt like she had been accepted by someone, then Sabine had to go and cruelly hurt her once again.

Sabine told her she must leave her family alone, she told her if the media ever realized that she had an illegitimate daughter, the memory of Harvey Bernard would be ruined forever. Marielle tried to tell her she just wanted to meet her family, but Sabine hung up on her.

Marielle didn't cancel her trip, though it had suddenly taken on a very different meaning to her. Sabine had acknowledged her privately, but she was afraid to introduce her to the family she had never got to be a part of. Sabine had told her she didn't want the past dredged up. What about my past? Thought Marielle.

Marielle made one last trip to her parents house in Mont

Legun before she left for Chicago. She had a quiet dinner with her parents that night but she felt tense there with her parents. They had never really been close, and their relationship had grown even more tense since her parents had confirmed that she was adopted and they had hid the truth from her for more than forty six years.

Marielle asked them why they had done that. Why had they hidden the truth from her for more than forty six years? Claudine explained to her that their extended families would not be able to handle the truth. They had been thrilled that Jean Paul and Claudine had married. It wasn't until their wedding night, that Claudine realized that a marriage to Jean Paul would never work, she had been fighting her feelings for years, she was not attracted to men and she never would be.

Of course, they couldn't just divorce, what would everyone think about that? They came to an agreement, they would stay married and each would fulfill their sexual needs however they saw fit, and the other would look the other way. Marielle shook her head in misery when she heard their story.

"Do you know how Papa fulfilled his needs?" cried Marielle, her voice breaking with pain.

"Yes," said Claudine, her voice was suddenly very meek and quiet. "What could I do? We had an agreement."

"I was seven years old!" cried Marielle, her face red with anger and disgust. Jean Paul was biting his lip, fighting tears.

Claudine looked away, she couldn't speak.

"How could you let him do that to me?" cried Marielle, standing and getting in her mother's face.

"There are worse things in life, than having a man make love to you," she snapped angrily. Marielle gasped and dragged in a ragged breath, she couldn't believe the woman who had raised her, could actually say such a thing. She was finally convinced that it was not love that she received, but her father's pent up lust.

"Then why did you not let him make love to you?" cried Marielle, standing up and stalking out of the house angrily. She couldn't believe it, neither of her parents really loved her, her very presence in the household had been all for appearances. Of course the Benoits and the Fortescue's thought that they were such a happy little family, but it was all a lie.

Marielle's anger was ready to eat her alive. She had meant nothing to these people. Her own father had used her to feed his own sick fantasies and her adopted mother had no desire to have Jean Paul make love to her, so she looked the other way when it was obvious to her that he was using his own daughter to fulfill his sexual needs.

Marielle got in her car to head back to Paris, she was done with these people. Why did she feel the need to love them, when obviously, they didn't love her? She sat there in her car waiting for the emotion to pass, but the tears wouldn't stop. She sat there in her car wondering why she was crying over these heartless people who obviously weren't worth her tears.

Finally, after the longest time she dried her tears and tried to collect her thoughts enough to find a place to stay the night. It was getting quite late and she didn't trust herself to drive all the way to Paris. She drove toward the center of town, then she had another thought. She could go back to the cottage and stay in her own room.

When she pulled back up to the bed and breakfast it was totally dark. There were no guests and Jean Paul and Claudine had obviously gone to bed. She parked her car and quietly let herself in the back door. She crept down the hall to her room. She was so tired and mentally drained, she fell asleep almost immediately.

Marielle awoke just after four a.m., panting and sweating profusely. It was her recurrent nightmare, waking up in the basement clinic in Paris and seeing her mutilated baby on the operating table. The doctor staring down at her reprovingly, telling her that her baby had been fine...they had murdered it.

The tears were streaming down Marielle's face as she flipped on the lights in the kitchen. She went to her mother's knife drawer and found the biggest knife they had.

She held it up to the light and inspected the shining blade carefully. She ran her finger down the blade to check the sharpness, it was perfect. She smiled a bit of an evil smile as she thought about her parents laying asleep in their bed and how they would never be able to hurt her again.

Jean Paul and Claudine had never loved her, she knew that now, and her own father had forced her to murder the one thing she wanted the most. Marielle was shaking uncontrollably and tears were streaming down her face as she entered her parents bedroom...

Chapter 24

Marielle was back on the little rise that allowed her a bird's eye view of Paloma's house, carefully monitoring the police presence in and around the house. She was sitting there in the tiny blue Focus with Montana license plates, not really worried at this point. They weren't looking for this car.

Unfortunately, she was going to have to come up with a new plan. Apparently the police were not as stupid as she had hoped they were. She was well aware that it was her credit card that had tipped them off, She hadn't wanted to use it, but she had run out of cash much faster than she had anticipated, gas was so expensive.

They had realized she was heading west on I-90, they might have guessed that she planned to pay her half sister a visit. Where else could she possibly be heading? She shook her head disgustedly, it just wasn't right, the little bitch had been born with a silver spoon in her mouth. She seemed to live a charmed life. She was now a respected physician, living in this upscale community in a gorgeous home of her own.

Marielle sneered. Her half sister had it all. She was beautiful and had an adoring family. She had grown up in a mansion, with a wealthy father who adored her. She probably slept in a bedroom fit for a princess as a child, never worrying that her father was going to call her to his bedroom. Never worrying that she would have to endure his sweaty body on top of her.

Marielle snapped to attention as the front door of the house opened. She watched carefully as Paloma came out, escorted by two police officers. Paloma looked exactly as she had expected her to. Her pale blonde hair was elegantly coiffed into a short bob and she was tall and slender, just like Marielle. She looked classy, just like her mother, she was wearing a black pencil skirt, heels and a light rain jacket as she followed the two police officers to the police car and got in.

The police car backed out of the driveway and Marielle followed, keeping a safe distance. Marielle wondered where they were going, perhaps to the police station for questioning. Marielle smiled, Paloma knew nothing of her, she doubted that Sabine had told anyone of their phone conversations, she was so worried about her damn reputation. Sabine Rousseau would never admit to the public that she'd had an illegitimate daughter, Marielle giggled to herself. All she had wanted was acceptance, now all the people who refused to accept her were dead...except Paloma.

Marielle kept a safe distance, as the police car wound through town and finally pulled up at the front entrance of Seattle Children's hospital.

Paloma and one officer got out of the police cruiser and went into the hospital. Marielle was panicking, she wanted to follow them, but she couldn't just abandon her car. If she parked illegally, she would be found out. She followed the signs that indicated the parking area and parked the car in the garage as quickly as she could.

When she was finally back in the hospital she looked around anxiously, trying to decide where Paloma might have gone to. She looked around at the throngs of people everywhere. She wasn't sure how she might find Paloma, in this huge hospital. She followed a hallway that went off to the left. She had no idea where she was going, she was merely acting on a feeling.

She passed a nurses station on the right. She looked the area over carefully, it appeared to be completely deserted. There was a white lab coat draped over one of the chairs and Marielle walked over and snatched it up, she continued down the hall, which eventually met a cross hall. She slipped the jacket on and looked cautiously down the cross hallway.

There was a bit more activity to her right, so she started walking that direction. The hallway led her to a busy main desk area. She walked up to a woman who was wearing a phone earpiece and seemed to be quite harried.

"I am Doctor Bell, I am here to consult with Dr. Webster. Can you tell me where I might find her?" asked Marielle, once again concealing her French accent with ease.

"Third floor, oncology," said the woman, barely acknowledging her existence.

"Thank you," said Marielle, nodding and heading toward the elevators.

She took the elevator up to the third floor. She looked around and followed the signs to the unit marked "Oncology". When she arrived on the Oncology unit, the nurses station was busy, but she did not see any sign of Paloma. She walked over to a desk and picked up a chart and began flipping through it slowly. It gave her a vantage point to watch everyone else around her, without drawing a lot of attention to herself. She seemed to be perfectly absorbed in her own world. Everyone was scurrying around doing their own thing, no one seemed to notice her at all.

"Can I help you?" asked a tiny voice.

Marielle wheeled around and saw a tiny oriental woman standing there. She was barely over five foot tall, her silky brown hair was pulled up in a pony tail and her piercing brown eyes were focused on Marielle. This small nurse was dressed in blue scrubs and was wearing a name tag that said; Tina Spaulding, RN.

"Hello nurse Spaulding, I am Dr. Bell. Dr. Webster contacted me about a patient she wants a consult on, may I speak to her?" asked Marielle, smiling sweetly.

"Oh, I think you may have just missed her. I believe she said she was going to medical records to catch up on her charts," said the nurse.

"Where is that?" asked Marielle.

"First floor, follow the signs. If there is no one at the

desk you can scan your name badge to get in the door," said nurse Spaulding.

"Thank you," said Marielle, sub consciously touching the name badge that she hadn't realized was dangling from the lapel of the lab jacket. She backed away slowly, then headed back toward the elevators. When she was safely in the elevator, with no one but a bent over, elderly woman with her, she was happy to realize that the name badge had spun around so that the name and picture had not been visible to nurse Spaulding. It was a good thing too. The name badge belonged to a Dr. Patel, who's picture revealed him to be an older looking, Indian man.

Marielle took the elevator down to the first floor and followed the signs to medical records. As luck would have it, there was no one at the desk so Marielle used the name badge to let herself in the door. She walked into the main room and was surprised to see a female police officer sitting at the desk. Other than that, the room appeared to be completely void of personnel.

The officer was was relaxed in her chair, completely engrossed in a game she was playing on her phone. She looked up and saw Marielle standing there. Marielle was holding her breath anxiously.

"Good afternoon doctor. Um, you're welcome to go about your business. I'm just hanging out, waiting for Dr. Webster," she said, pointing up at a sign labeled; "doctor's dictation". She was so distracted, she barely gave Marielle a second glance.

"Oh, have a good day then," said Marielle, smiling sweetly.

"Yeah, you too," said the woman, barely looking up from her game.

Marielle smiled to herself and followed the signs to Doctor's dictation, she almost giggled at the thought of Paloma's protector, barely paying attention at all. She had just let her walk on by, with barely a second glance.

Marielle opened the door of the doctor's dictation room and was excited to see Paloma sitting at a desk with her back to the door. She had the phone to her ear and she was dictating a report into the phone. She was completely oblivious that anyone was in the room with her.

Marielle took a deep breath and pulled the hunting knife from her purse. She stifled a giggle, this was going to be too easy. She could slit Paloma's throat in a matter of seconds and she would be completely silenced. The police officer in the other room would probably never hear a thing. It would be bloody, but it would be fast and easy. She would probably not escape from the hospital, as she would most likely be completely covered in blood, but there was no reason to escape. Her life was over anyway...no one loved her.

Her work would be done, Paloma would be dead. There was no reason to cut Paloma's heart out...leave a message...the circle would be complete.

Chapter 25

Bellamy had a bad feeling deep in his gut. He had no idea how long Marielle could have been stalking the Webster family but now he knew she could have been doing it all completely undetected, they had all been looking for the wrong car.

The Seattle police were on high alert now, but he hoped that all the officers didn't have the same nonchalant attitude that the officer at the house had. He was exasperated with the whole situation, for some reason, he was the only one who seemed to see Marielle for what she was...a very dangerous criminal.

He now had his own rental car, so he drove to Seattle Children's Hospital like a bat out of hell. En route, he had called and talked to the Chief of the Seattle police and told him his concerns. Even the chief himself had been way too laid back for Bellamy's taste. The chief told him that he had provided Paloma with a police escort, what else could he possibly do?

He told Bellamy himself that he thought he was overreacting. There was no reason to believe that Marielle was after Paloma and so far, no one had even seen the blue focus or Marielle Benoit. The entire Settle police department was assuming she was still in Montana somewhere.

Bellamy pulled into the parking garage and began looping around, looking for a parking spot. The garage was claustrophobic and crowded with cars. He followed the arrows around and around the levels in the dim light as he rounded a corner, he noticed a car that was parked haphazardly.

So haphazardly, in fact, that there wasn't room for anyone to park on one side, it stood out to Bellamy mainly because the car itself was tiny. Bellamy almost cruised right past the car in his quest to find a space, then he squinted at the car in shock. The garage was poorly lit, but it was obvious the car he was looking at, was a blue Ford Focus with Montana license plates.

Bellamy stopped his car abruptly and pulled his notepad from his pocket. He gazed down at the license plate number he had jotted down on the pad. A 17699.

He stared at the car in shock with his mouth hanging open. Marielle was here. He dialed the number for the Seattle police department and asked for the chief, he was put on hold. His heart was pounding with adrenaline and he was suddenly worried that he might be too late.

He pulled his car around to where the elevators were and slammed it into park, he jumped out of the car and headed for the elevators. He couldn't waste anymore time looking for a parking space. Marielle was here, and so was Paloma. He could only hope that he could find Paloma before Marielle did.

He was still on hold waiting for the chief. His phone was crackling in protest of the poor reception in the thick concrete parking garage. The elevators took him to the main lobby of the hospital which was bright and teaming with people. Bellamy was trying to shake off his confusion as he looked around the bustling lobby, trying to figure out which way to go.

"Mangold," snapped the voice on the other end of the line, finally.

"This is Detective Bellamy with the Chicago Police. I'm at Seattle Children's Hospital. I just saw Marielle Benoit's car in the parking garage, the blue Ford Focus. She's here," cried Bellamy, it was hard to keep his voice in check, his heart was pounding and he could feel the adrenaline charging through his body.

"Benoit is there? At the hospital?" cried Chief Mangold.

"Yes, I need everyone you've got here quickly, she's dangerous," said Bellamy.

"Got it," said the chief, hanging up the phone.

Bellamy was still looking around, the hospital was massive, he had no idea where to go. He saw a sign that said; "information", so he headed that direction.

The information desk was buzzing. He walked up to the desk, a woman wearing a telephone headpiece seemed to be very busy. She gave him a harried smile.

"Can I help you?"

"I'm looking for Dr. Paloma Webster," said Bellamy.

"Third floor, oncology," said the woman, in her practiced, monotone voice.

Bellamy headed for the elevators and took them up to the third floor, he headed toward the section marked, "Oncology". He stood at the nurses station, glancing around completely lost. There was lots of staff, but he didn't see Paloma Webster anywhere. In moments, he was catching glances of Seattle uniforms arriving on the floor. It was as if they'd come out of the woodwork.

There were at least six of them and they seemed to be doing a systematic search of the floor, which made Bellamy feel a little bit better, though he wouldn't be happy till he actually found Paloma or Marielle...it made no difference which at this point, as long as Paloma was still alive.

The nurses station was buzzing and crowded with staff. There were more than a dozen nurses and physicians all busy with phone calls and patient charts. The drone of their conversations and the seemingly constant ringing of the phones was almost unnerving to Bellamy. He finally managed to get the attention of a slightly rotund nurse with red hair who was sitting nearby, tapping away at a computer.

"Excuse me, I'm looking for Dr. Webster. Have you seen her?" asked Bellamy.

The woman frowned, she was obviously overwhelmed but Bellamy didn't care. This was a matter of life and death.

"She was here earlier. I have no idea where she went,"

said the woman, shaking her head with barely concealed disdain.

"Last I heard, she was going to medical records, at least that's where I sent Dr. Bell," said nurse Spaulding, who was standing several feet away, with a phone to her ear.

"Who's doctor Bell?" asked Bellamy.

"I don't know, she said Dr. Webster consulted her, I've never seen her before. If her hair had been shorter, I actually, might have mistaken her for Dr. Webster. It was weird, they look a lot alike," said nurse Spaulding.

"Holy shit!" cried Bellamy.

He ran toward the uniforms that were currently making a search of the floor. He flashed them his badge and introduced himself to them.

"We need to go to medical records, Dr. Webster is there, and apparently a nurse just sent a Dr. Bell, there. I am sure that Dr. Bell, is Marielle Benoit," said Bellamy, his heart suddenly sinking. He could only hope that Paloma was still alive. Marielle Benoit had found her and he was certain that her police escort wouldn't be enough to stop Marielle from finishing her deadly mission.

The adrenaline was coursing through Bellamy's veins as he ran toward the elevator. His entire body was filled with dread, he could only hope they weren't too late.

JEAN MARIE STANBERRY

Chapter 26

Paloma's heart was heavy as she dictated her progress note on Kayla Stevenson. She had done everything possible, but she was certain Kayla had only hours left in this lifetime. The one positive was that Kayla was ready. She knew her fate and somehow, she had made peace with it. Even her parents had recently come to the realization that they had done everything, but still, their little girl was going to leave them.

Paloma heard the door to the dictation room open, she didn't turn around. She could see a white coated woman out of the corner of her eye. It was that time of the month, everyone was being summoned to medical records to get their charts in order, it was that or loose your hospital privileges until the work was done. The end of the month usually had all the physicians scrambling.

The medical records room was quiet and isolated. Paloma had been a bit spooked to come back here, knowing her half sister whom she had never even met, was out there somewhere with intentions of murdering her. The room would never allow for an escape, there was only that one entrance, she would be at a disadvantage if Marielle Benoit were to find her here. Paloma wasn't too worried, her police escort was out front, how could Marielle ever get to her?

Paloma had been a bit anxious when she had left the house this morning. She had never required a police escort before. Now apparently, the police believed that her half sister, whom she had never even met, was out to get her. The very thought was a bit overwhelming. What had she ever done to this woman?

Paloma shuddered a bit, her stomach was suddenly turning with a sense of dread she had never felt in her entire life. She could suddenly feel the hair on the back of her neck standing up. She turned around slowly to take a look at the woman who had just entered the room. Her heart began to accelerate as she realized the woman who had entered the room was not a doctor, as she had originally assumed, but her half sister Marielle.

The woman, in her white lab coat, was walking slowly toward her. Her pale skin was marred by dark circles under her eyes, a testament to the hours she had spent on the road in her quest to get here. Her face was expressionless and she was holding a large hunting knife, which she was raising slowly as she approached. Paloma drew in a deep, shaky breath as Marielle flashed her an evil smile when she saw the stunned look on her face.

"Marielle?" asked Paloma, her own voice seemed far away and her heart was racing at an exhausting pace. It was inevitable, of course, when you knew the person you were speaking to, planned to murder you.

"Bonjour," said Marielle, smiling sweetly at her.

"Why have you come all this way? What do you want from me?" cried Paloma, trying not to shrink away. In her mind, she had already decided that she was not going to go down without a fight. She had children who needed her and a husband who adored her, she planned to do anything she could, to avoid being a victim. Paloma took a deep, shaky breath, she was trying to formulate a plan in her head. Unfortunately, Marielle had the element of surprise. Paloma was essentially trapped there without a weapon, there was no other way out of the room, Marielle was blocking the only exit.

"I want nothing from you. You have already taken the life that was rightfully mine," snapped Marielle.

"I cannot help who I am. I was not responsible for your pain," said Paloma. She did not doubt that Marielle had a hard life, but she was not at fault, she had been an innocent victim herself.

"Do you have any idea what I went through? Being left behind with him! Do you have any idea what he did to me, his own flesh and blood?" cried Marielle.

"Your father abused you?" asked Paloma, acutely aware that she needed to keep Marielle talking. Maybe if she could talk to her, be a friend to her, that her own pain would end this.

"It was so much more than that. I would have relished it, had he just beat me, but it was much worse than that. When I was seven he started having sex with me. I was just a little girl!" cried Marielle, she was dangerously close to breaking down in tears.

"You were only seven?" Paloma almost shuddered, no wonder this poor woman was so screwed up. "I'm so sorry. Can you tell me about it?" asked Paloma, offering her a wry smile and kind eyes. This woman was in pain more than anything, she needed to be heard.

"I thought he loved me, he told me that he loved me...more than any other papa loved their little girl...I was scared," breathed Marielle, her stunning blue eyes were vacant.

"Of course you were, you were a child," said Paloma, her voice was soft and soothing.

"I knew it was wrong when he was touching me, when he was taking my clothes off...but he told me it was okay," sniffled Marielle.

"It wasn't your fault. He was your father, he was supposed to be your protector. Your response to him was natural, he was your parent, a man you've been told your entire life you must obey. He used your trust against you," said Paloma.

"Yes, I trusted him...I wanted him to love me. After a while, it didn't seem wrong any more. I wanted it, I looked forward to it. It was the only love that anyone gave me in that house. My mother Claudine never loved me, in fact, I believe she detested me," said Marielle.

"All children want to be loved, it was not your fault at all. You needed someone to care about you," said Paloma, watching her carefully. Marielle was holding the knife, but her hand was shaking. Paloma hoped she was close to breaking down, maybe it would give her a chance to get away.

"When I was seventeen I got pregnant. I tried to hide it, because I wanted the baby. Papa figured it out soon enough, he insisted that I get an abortion, even though it was so late in my pregnancy. We went to a doctor in Paris, we ended up in a basement somewhere, it was dirty and scary. I went to sleep and when I woke up...oh God...it was awful," cried Marielle, her body suddenly raked with sobs.

"What happened when you woke up?" asked Paloma, gently prodding her, as Marielle sobbed uncontrollably.

"When I woke up, I saw the baby on the table, only the doctor had ripped the baby to shreds when he took it out. I cried and cried when I saw that baby. Not to mention the fact that I was in horrible pain. I bled and bled and almost died. I couldn't tell Claudine what was wrong with me. My papa had warned me, if I told anyone, he would deny everything," said Marielle.

"I'm so sorry, how horrible for you," said Paloma.

"How would you know, you stupid slut? You had everything! Your family loved you!" cried Marielle, her face suddenly twisted into a mask of cold anger. Paloma took in a deep, shaky breath, she wanted the attention off of her and back on Marielle's pain.

"Yes, I was lucky. My father did love me, but my mother didn't love me, I was a mistake, she never really wanted me," said Paloma.

"I don't believe that...I saw you on TV, I saw everything," said Marielle, seething.

"It was all an act. I swear to you that my mother didn't want me, she was not the loving mother she seemed to be on TV. I too, was an accident, but Harvey wanted children so badly, he would never allow my mother to have an abortion, even though she was afraid her body would never be the same and her career would be over.

When I was older, five or six, she decided that I was marketable, but still, she only wanted me around when she thought I could be useful to her.

Harvey adored all his children, but his love for us only made our situation with my mother worse. She didn't like sharing Harvey, she needed to be the center of attention at all times so she felt like we were taking his attention away from her. It was horrible, you have no idea," said Paloma.

"At least your father truly loved you. I was...I was nothing but an object," said Marielle, her lip was quivering.

"I'm very sorry, it hurts to be used like that," said Paloma, carefully monitoring the tone of her voice, she was trying to keep the tone low and emotionless, it was hard...she was scared.

"Yes," said Marielle, her lip was quivering, she had lowered the knife, it was at her side now. Paloma was holding out hope that she could convince her to drop it and end all of this peacefully.

"Please. I wish we could be friends," said Paloma, watching her carefully.

"Why would you want to be my friend?" asked Marielle, assessing her suspiciously. Paloma could feel the perspiration sliding down her back, there was only one way out of this room and it was through Marielle. She was so close now...

"Well the obvious...we're sisters. I really always wanted a sister. I mean, Patrice is my sister but we were never close, there's a twenty year age difference between us. She's more like a child to me than a sister. But you and I, we have a lot to talk about. I mean, I feel like I know you, even though we've never met before," said Paloma.

"I feel like I know you too," said Marielle. She took a slow step toward Paloma. Paloma wanted to shrink back in fear, but the knife was still at Marielle's side, she didn't seem to be a threat at this point.

Paloma jumped when she heard shouting in the room down the hall. There were footsteps in the hallway and Marielle had suddenly wheeled around, raising her knife defensively.

Bellamy skidded into the doorway, followed by three uniformed officers. His gun was drawn and he was pointing it at Marielle, as were the other three officers.

"Freeze!" shouted Bellamy.

Marielle seemed confused. She now had four guns in her face and she was standing there, frozen in confusion.

Paloma had backed up against the desk and was standing there, staring at them in shock.

"I want you out!" cried Marielle, glaring at the four officers in front of her. There were four guns, all pointed at her, yet she appeared to be unmoved. "I am speaking with my sister!"

"Drop the knife!" shouted Bellamy. His body was tingling with the adrenaline that was charging through his veins. Marielle seemed to be surrendering, but he was worried it was a trick, he wanted the knife out of her hands.

"Paloma, you are right, none of this was your fault. Please, take the knife," said Marielle, turning and offering the knife to Paloma.

Paloma was frozen for a second, then she took one resolute step toward Marielle.

"No!" cried Bellamy. "Do not approach her Paloma. It's a trick!"

"Paloma?" gasped Marielle, her voice was thick with emotion.

"Marielle! I want you to drop the knife! Drop the knife on the floor and kick it toward me." cried Bellamy. He took a step toward them, hoping to place his body in front of the other three officers. They were young and way too nervous. He was having a bad feeling about this confrontation.

Marielle turned and gave him an arrogant glare, then she took another step toward Paloma. Bellamy was beginning to panic. It was entirely possible that this was a trick. What if Marielle pretended that she had made he peace with Paloma, but it was a ruse. It was possible she still planned to jump Paloma and stab her as they watched.

"I said, drop the knife! Do it or I'll shoot!" cried Bellamy, steadying his finger on the trigger. He just wanted the knife out of her hands.

"Please Marielle, do what he says," breathed Paloma, her voice was fading away and she was visibly shaking.

"Paloma," said Marielle, holding the knife out to her, as if it were a special gift.

Paloma swallowed anxiously and took another tentative step toward her half sister. Bellamy, was nervous. He didn't know what kind of encounter the sisters had experienced, but they seemed to have called a truce, though he still wasn't sure he could trust Marielle.

"Paloma, not another step. I want her to drop the knife!" cried Bellamy, the crack in his voice betrayed the fear he was feeling.

"Marielle, he wants you to drop the knife," said Paloma, her voice was firm, but faint.

"I want to, but he's going to kill me," said Marielle, looking into Bellamy's eyes.

"I'm not going to kill you, I want you to drop the knife," said Bellamy, his voice was taunt, like a tightly stretched wire.

"Please Marielle, just drop the knife," said Paloma, her voice breaking nervously. The only other sound in the room was the creaking of leather, it was the gun belts of three uniformed police officers who were standing there with their guns drawn, waiting for the moment Marielle would drop the knife, or give them a reason to start shooting.

Marielle spun around nervously and held out her arms to Paloma, in a gesture of fear. She was lost, she didn't know what to do. Paloma just stood there numbly, not knowing what to do. The room was completely silent, except for the restless creaking of the leather.

"I'm going to count to three," said Bellamy, calmly.

Marielle shot him a panicked look, then she turned and looked at Paloma anxiously. Paloma nodded her head calmly, willing her to just drop the knife. Her heart was pounding furiously, she just wanted this to end. Marielle was so close to giving in...

"One."

Marielle looked into Bellamy's eyes, she seemed confused, her hands were shaking.

"Two."

"Marielle...please," said Paloma, pleading with her eyes.

"Three." said Bellamy, looking Marielle in the eye.

Marielle took a deep breath and turned her body to face Bellamy, she looked down at the knife in resignation, opening her hand slowly. Just as Bellamy was sure Marielle was going to drop the knife, there was a deafening shot. It was a moment that was inconceivably short, but seemed to last an eternity.

Paloma looked at her sister in awe, as a strange black hole in Marielle's forehead erupted into a torrent of blood. Her sister gave her a stunned look and the knife fell to the floor. Marielle stood there for that eternity, unmoving. Then, as blood began to trickle into her right eye, she reached up and touched the wound, her fingers now covered in her own blood.

Bellamy had wheeled around to see where the shot had come from. He knew instantly it had come from the gun of the female officer who had been in charge of Paloma's protection. The other officers were staring at her in shock ,as the seconds ticked by.

Marielle wobbled and then fell to the floor, Paloma ran to her and cradled her head in her lap.

"What is wrong with you? She was surrendering!" cried Paloma, angrily, her accusing eyes on the female officer.

"She was raising the knife, she was going to kill you!" cried the female officer, her face was flushed and her voice was breaking with emotion.

In moments the room was filled with people. It was buzzing with voices. Paloma sat on the floor with Marielle's head cradled in her arms. She was covered in Marielle's blood and she cried, as her half sister died in her arms.

Bellamy frowned, as he watched the two women bonding for the first time as Marielle's life slipped away. In a perfect world, the two of them could have been happy together. Sisters...so much alike, but raised in two different worlds.

Bellamy sighed a miserable sigh and turned to leave. Sometimes solving a crime was not as satisfying as it might seem.

ABOUT THE AUTHOR

Jean Marie Stanberry lives in northwest Montana with her husband of twenty five years, their children Ryan and Lauren and their golden retriever Molly.

Jean works full time as a nurse in surgery but she also enjoys writing, figure skating, kayaking, cross country skiing, hiking, gardening and gourmet cooking.

The family loves to travel and Jean loves to use her travel experiences as an inspiration for her writing.